IRON STAR

BOOKS BY LOREN D. ESTLEMAN

AMOS WALKER MYSTERIES

Motor City Blue

Angel Eyes

The Midnight Man

The Glass Highway

Sugartown

Every Brilliant Eye

Lady Yesterday

Downriver

Silent Thunder

Sweet Women Lie

Never Street

The Witchfinder

The Hours of the Virgin

*A Smile on the Face of
the Tiger*

Sinister Heights

Poison Blonde*

Retro*

Nicotine Kiss*

American Detective*

The Left-Handed Dollar*

Infernal Angels*

Burning Midnight*

Don't Look for Me*

You Know Who Killed Me*

The Sundown Speech*

The Lioness Is the Hunter*

Black and White Ball*

*When Old Midnight Comes
Along**

Cutthroat Dogs*

Monkey in the Middle*

City Walls*

VALENTINO, FILM DETECTIVE

Frames*

Alone*

Alive! *

Shoot*

Brazen*

Indigo*

Vamp*

DETROIT CRIME

Whiskey River

Motown

King of the Corner

Edsel

Stress

Jitterbug*

Thunder City*

PETER MACKLIN

Kill Zone

Roses Are Dead

Any Man's Death

*Something Borrowed,
Something Black**

Little Black Dress*

*Published by Tor Publishing Group

IRON STAR

LOREN D. ESTLEMAN

TOR PUBLISHING GROUP

NEW YORK

IRON STAR

Copyright © 2024 by Loren D. Estleman

A Forge Book
Published by Tom Doherty Associates / Tor Publishing Group
120 Broadway
New York, NY 10271

www.torpublishinggroup.com

Forge® is a registered trademark of Macmillan Publishing Group, LLC.

The Library of Congress Cataloging-in-Publication Data
is available upon request.

ISBN 978-1-250-89251-5 (hardcover)
ISBN 978-1-250-89252-2 (ebook)

Our books may be purchased in bulk for promotional, educational,
or business use. Please contact your local bookseller or the
Macmillan Corporate and Premium Sales Department
at 1-800-221-7945, extension 5442, or by email at
MacmillanSpecialMarkets@macmillan.com.

First Edition: 2024

Printed in the United States of America

0 9 8 7 6 5 4 3 2 1

For Dominick Abel
with deep appreciation

The end of man is knowledge.

—Robert Penn Warren,
All the King's Men

I

MISTER ST. JOHN

1

MR. JONES

Everything about the messenger seemed smart, from the peaked cap squared across his brow to the polished toes of his boots, right down to the smug cast of his mouth. Rawlings signed for the package he brought and handed back the clipboard; and bless the man if he didn't snap him a salute. He shut the door on the pink clean-shaven face and went to his desk for the knife that was too big for its purpose.

The cord severed, he removed two layers of brown paper and looked at the book. A phantom pain struck his side.

The book was standard octavo size but heavy as a brick, coarse brittle pages bound in green cloth with a surplus of stamping on cover and spine and the kind of lettering one found in soap advertisements. A balloon legend at the top descended in graded diminuendo until the second-to-last line, which was set out boldly in copper leaf:

THE IRON STAR
Being a Memoir of IRONS ST. JOHN
Deputy U.S. Marshal
Peace Officer
Railroad Detective
Trail-blazer
And

CANDIDATE FOR U.S. CONGRESS
by Himself

The educated reader might have added *Reformed Out-law* to the list of sobriquets—with a Christian nod to the "Reformed"—but the object of the tome had been to elect, not repent. In fact it had managed to do neither, thus setting in motion the cosmic chain of events that had pulled Rawlings into his orbit.

Another stab came when he opened to the frontispiece, a three-quarter photographic portrait of a man past his middle years. It was contemporary to his experience of the original, although the developers' art had tightened the sagging lines of the chin: a rectangular face set off by cheekbones that threatened to pierce the flesh and a thick moustache whose points reached nearly to the corners of the jaw. The eyes had been retouched as well, but less to flatter the subject than to keep them from washing out in the glare from the flashpan; irises that particular shade of sunned steel did not reproduce. The hair was cut to the shape of the skull and swept across the forehead; that feature, Rawlings thought, had not been tampered with. In all the weeks he'd spent with the man—seldom more than six feet away—he could barely recall having seen him with his hat off: Cavalry campaign issue, it was, stained black around the base of the dimpled crown, with the tassel missing a toggle.

It was like finding an old ogre of a dead uncle standing on his doorstep.

The book carried a 1906 copyright date and the name of a St. Louis publisher. He touched the page, as if feeling the figures pressed into paper would contradict the evidence of sight, and also of scent; the leaves smelled of dust and decomposition.

Twenty years.

He was fifty, the same age St. John had been then, when the man had seemed as weatherworn as the Red Wall of Wyoming.

The old humbug.

But, no; that was unfair. You didn't mark down a man's accomplishments just because he never missed an opportunity to remind you of them. He'd been a politician after all, however briefly and unsuccessfully, and that wound had yet to heal. Was he so easily dismissed as less than advertised? Truth to tell, constant exposure for nearly a month to any fellow creature outdoors in all extremes of weather would turn an Ivanhoe into a Uriah Heep. There were no heroes in a cold camp.

He turned to the first page of the editor's preface. ("Nothing in little Ike's childhood bore witness to the man he would become.") Tucked in the seam between the sawtooth sheets was a cardboard rectangle, glaringly white against the ivory pulp, with glossy black embossed printing in eleven-point type:

CHARLES GEBHARDT, ESQ.

The card contained neither address nor telephone number: a proper gentleman's calling card, an anomaly there, amidst the oat and barley fields of southeastern Minnesota.

Likewise there was no return address on the wrapper, and no postmark, since it had been sent by private messenger; nothing to explain its origin apart from the unfamiliar name on the card, which may have been nothing other than a bookmark employed by a former owner. The book was sufficiently shopworn to have passed from hand to hand, eventually to settle in a clearance bin, the last stop before the pulp mill. No provenance, and not an inkling as to purpose.

But he was still enough of a detective not to waste time pursuing a line of reasoning that offered no beginning and promised no end. He laid aside the book and took a seat in the wooden armchair that had come with the room, at the leftward-listing rolltop that had come with it, and turned back a cuff to measure his pulse against his watch.

After fifteen seconds he took his fingers from his wrist, replaced the cuff, fixed the stud, and entered the figure in the notebook he kept in a pigeonhole.

Not too rapid, considering; but on the other hand his heart wasn't likely to finish out of the money at the Olmsted County Fair. He snapped shut the face of the watch, glancing from habit at the engraving but without reading: TO EMMETT FORCE RAWLINGS, IN GRATEFUL, ETC., ROBT. PINKERTON II, and returned it to his waistcoat pocket, where the weight of the gold plate tugged the unbuttoned garment uncomfortably off-center. He fastened the buttons.

From the right drawer he lifted a stack of yellow paper and reread what he'd written in the same small, precise hand he'd employed while waiting out his retirement in the records room in San Francisco. He reread it from the beginning as always, scratching out passages that struck him as prosy and inserting additional information in the margins, which he'd left wide for the purpose. The Chief had often said that if he ever tired of the field he could apply for a post in bookkeeping; after the Buckner debacle the remark had seemed not so much a compliment as a threat.

He caught himself stroking his chin; there'd been no beard there for years. That blasted book had sidetracked him. One of the reasons he'd started this comprehensive history of the

Agency was to expel the nattering memories of his past, as well as to audit the account.

The Wild West: No grand exposition, that: rather a roadside carnival. Hundreds of hacks had squandered tons of paper and gallons of ink on midnight rides and gunplay; which, if one were to lift them from the record, would have no effect on how it had come out. Dakota would have been divided, the Indian question resolved, and the frontier closed regardless of which side emerged intact from the O.K. Corral fight, whether William Bonney was slain from ambush or escaped to old Mexico, or if Buffalo Bill had chosen black tie and tails over feathers and buckskin. Washington was the big top, Tombstone and Deadwood a sideshow at best. Historians were crows, hopping over treasure to snatch up bright scraps of tin and deposit them at the feet of spectators who— thanks to them—would never know the difference.

His face ached; the scowl might have set permanently but for the interruption of a tap on his door. He shoved himself away from the desk and got up to answer it.

"A gentleman to see you, sir." Mrs. Balfour, his landlady, extended a card in a large hand with veins on the back as thick as a man's. She was a tall Scot who held her hair fast with glittering pins and kept snuff in a hinged locket around her neck.

He took the card, read again the name Charles Gebhardt, Esq. "I don't suppose he said what he wants."

"No, sir, and it wasn't my business to ask."

In truth he couldn't imagine what circumstances would lead this woman to ask any sort of question, including whether she should allow the man up. They exchanged meaningless nods and she went back downstairs.

He remained in the doorway while the visitor ascended

the last flight. At the top they stood not quite face to face; the man was two inches shorter and thicker in the torso, with a nose straight as a plumb and big ears that stuck out like spread clamshells. His smile was broad as well, overabundantly friendly, and furnished with teeth too white and even for trust: a salesman's smile. Larger-than-life features on a larger-than-life head. They belonged on a billboard.

The hat was wrong: a tweed motoring cap, worn at an angle after the current fashion, taking up too little space in relation to the head; and now that Rawlings had identified the problem, he realized where he'd seen the man, or at least his image, painted in crude brush strokes reproduced in lithograph: a muscular frame in blue denim, plaid flannel, and yellow kerchief, dangling from the face of a cliff or a railroad boxcar plummeting down a steep grade with no train attached. Perhaps both. Wearing the hat, too big just to provide shade and too small for a fire pit.

"Mr. Rawlings?" A pleasant enough voice, a tenor, with a hint of the stage.

"Mr.—Gebhardt?" The name was as unlikely a fit as the headgear.

The smile flickered. "Yes; but that's just between you, me, and the Bureau of Internal Revenue. Professionally it's Buck Jones, and I've come all this way from Los Angeles to ask if you'd consider making a movie with me."

2

PIG'S FEET AND A PROPOSITION

That settled the point. The man looked larger than life because he was: His image was projected across the country (and, for all Rawlings knew, around the world) on screens the size of tennis courts, every pore on that impossibly straight nose visible to the eye, and every bit in proportion to the preposterous hat, one that no stunt—a leap from a balcony, a barroom brawl, a horseback plunge down a perpendicular cliff—could dislodge.

"Mr. Jones—"

The visitor wasn't listening. His glance around the room was not so much contemptuous as angry; as if a figure so eminent as the former Pinkerton should be so overlooked by providence in his golden years. His unwilling host was suddenly conscious of the condition of his rug, of the bed that swung up into the wall when he bothered to make it.

Jones brightened. "Eaten yet? I've been living on hamburger sandwiches and canned corned beef for three days. They tell me the German food in this part's good. I grew up on Schnitzel and dumplings. My treat."

"I'm not hungry."

"Then you can watch me, and I'll buy the drinks. What's the dry situation here?"

Rawlings laughed.

* * *

The house was a Queen Anne, built by a lumber baron and cut up into apartments after his death; under Mrs. Balfour's ownership, the variegated colors of the siding had vanished beneath coats of leaden-gray paint. A great ferry boat of an automobile had come aground against the curb in front, enameled in brown and cream, chromium-trimmed, with white sidewalls, all reduced to a uniform tan by the dust of six states. Rawlings stopped short at the sight. "Your car?"

"Borrowed it from Tom Mix," Jones said. "Damned decent of him, considering Bill Fox only hired me to club down his salary. I think he wants to put some miles on it before he trades it in for something more grand; an ocean liner, I guess."

The seat that wrapped itself around the passenger's back and hips was upholstered in cowhide, with the hair still on. The dashboard was padded in brown leather and a pair of handstraps shaped like stirrups dangled from the roof.

Jones followed the course of his guest's eyes. "Think that's bad? I stopped overnight in Reno to get the steer horns taken off the hood and put in the trunk. The president's train draws less attention." He stepped on the starter. The motor cleared its throat twice and settled into a mumbling throb. "You're the navigator, Captain. Where to?"

Rawlings winced. That title—"Cap'n," actually—was the exclusive property of a man long dead. "St. Paul; there's nothing decent around here. I usually take the train, but I think I know where to tell you to turn."

"You don't drive?"

"I'm off automobiles. I had a bad experience once."

They followed the Mississippi north and crossed the bridge.

Minneapolis and St. Paul, settled by German immigrants

whose descendants were still very much in evidence, supported three Old Heidelbergs, each independently owned. The one Rawlings selected overlooked the two-hundred-foot gorge separating the Twin Cities, bleeding red iron in streaks down its gray face. Inside the Tudor construction, the beamed ceiling hung low over heavy oak wainscoting and high-backed booths, but there were no ornamental steins on shelves or Black Forest hunting prints on the walls. Jones commented on this.

"A band of patriots with flat feet set fire to the place during the war," Rawlings said. "They took issue with Sauerkraut on the menu instead of Liberty Cabbage. You can see some of the wood's still charred. The management got rid of the decorations, but kept the Kraut. I took you at your word when you said you wanted authentic German. Even the Original Old Heidelberg across the river serves chicken cacciatore; calling it *Hünchen* Bismarck doesn't fool anyone."

"Did you serve in the war?"

"No."

When nothing else was forthcoming, Jones said, "You didn't miss anything. I was in that mess in the Philippines; took a Moro slug in the leg. Last time out I broke horses in Chicago for the army. Goddamn waste of good horseflesh, that one."

"If you say so. I haven't ridden in years."

A bullet-headed waiter came to take their orders: pickled pig's feet with plenty of ketchup for Jones, Rawlings a plain turkey breast. The smells from the kitchen had stirred his appetite.

"And a set-up for me." Jones slapped his chest, striking something solid—plainly a flask—in an inside pocket. "Driving's thirsty work. You?"

"I don't drink."

The waiter cleared his throat and leaned close to the actor's ear. His breath smelled of vinegar. "We have a fine selection of beers and liquors, and the best wine cellar east of San Francisco."

"It's a wide-open town," Rawlings told his companion. "Courtesy of Police Chief O'Connor. In St. Paul, you step aside to give a highbinder the street."

"In that case, bring me a Lager dark enough to blot out the sun." Jones handed back his menu.

Rawlings did the same. "Mineral water."

"Ulcers?" asked Jones when they were alone.

"No."

"Hold 'em close to the chin, don't you?"

"You said something about making a movie. I assume that's the same thing as a photoplay."

"It is and I did. Seen many?"

"As a matter of fact I saw my first one last month, when my publisher was in town. I couldn't very well get out of it. A pirate slid down a mainsail on the end of a sword. I fell asleep before he broke any bones."

"I heard you were writing a book. That's why I thought of you."

"Where could you possibly have heard that? I don't have a contract yet. It's held up waiting for permission from Pinkerton's. They're afraid I'll sell trade secrets."

"You don't know Hollywood. It gobbles up ideas like a whale plowing through minnows and still it's hungry. Any time something breaks the surface that sounds like it'd make a pitch, the studios are on it like buzzards. My bet is Zukor will know the decision before you do. That's why I came all this way, to sew you up before someone beats me to the finish."

The waiter returned carrying a tray high above his head. He set a plate of glistening pig's feet in front of Jones, home-made ketchup in a small crock, and a steaming bowl of Sauer-kraut. Rawlings' turkey breast came divided into even slices with a sprig of parsley. A sudden stab of greedy hunger annoyed him; his system could not abide Kraut, but the smell of it always stirred his digestive juices.

A heavy glass mug contained liquid as black as pine pitch with a head of crackling foam. At a nod from Jones, the waiter scraped a half-inch off the top with a butter knife. He placed a glass of water in front of Rawlings and left with a bow; did it come with just the slightest hint of a heel click? All the man needed was a *Pökelsticher* helmet and puttees. It was a lesson in history how quickly a war could be forgotten.

The man from Hollywood spooned ketchup generously over his meal. "The frontier's in demand," he said. "*The Iron Horse* put Fox back on the map after Theda Bara fell on her face, and the old man's been buying up desert land like it's New York City real estate for location shooting. Famous Players is starring Bill Hart in *The Virginian*, and I guess I don't have to tell you what *Riders of the Purple Sage* did for Tom Mix."

"Yet you do. I've been up to my chin in old case files for months, and Mix isn't in any of them." Rawlings was busy cutting his turkey into bite-size cubes.

"Well, it did plenty. The studio turned right around and starred him in the sequel. Zane Grey's rolling in it; he could sell 'em a pair of socks out of that trunk of his and they'd never know the difference."

"My congratulations to Mr. Grey. I don't see what any of this has to do with me. I don't write fiction."

"That's just what I'm coming to. The way things are going,

the business will run out of made-up stories. Meanwhile the real thing's just laying there waiting for somebody to break ground. Mark my words; six months from now you won't be able to kick a can across any lot in L.A. without hitting some actor got up like Billy the Kid or Jesse James or *any* of the Daltons."

"I'm not surprised. Oscar Wilde said Americans always take their heroes from the criminal classes."

"Maybe so, but there are only so many bandits and killers. When that bucket's empty they're going to have to go to the other side of the badge. I'm getting together my own production company, and we mean to beat the studios to the trough. I've got Bob Steele on board, and Hoot Gibson says he's interested. What do you think of that?"

"I don't; because I don't know most of these names you're throwing around."

"Hear me out." Jones put aside his knife and fork and leaned forward to cup his hands around his beer. "I found *The Iron Star* on the ten-cent table in a shop in Long Beach; I remembered the name St. John from the wire columns back in Indiana. I took the book home and finished it in one sitting."

"That's impressive. I couldn't get through it twenty years ago, and I was under orders to read it."

"Oh, I skipped past the politics. He lost, the trusts won, and who cares? He didn't write it, not that part anyway. Did you get a chance to look it over again?"

"You were too eager. I barely got it unwrapped."

Jones blew a gust of air sharp with Kraut. "Hell, I could've brought it myself and saved the three-cent stamp. I underlined the parts I'm sure he wrote, or did before some English snob tore the guts out of it back in St. Louis. Riding for Parker, shooting it out with Jack LeFever, siding Heck Thomas in the hunt for Dick Spanish; that's all St. John. No party hack could get that across like someone who was there."

"He trapped beaver with Daniel Boone, too," Rawlings said. "Of course, he was drunk when he told me that."

Jones wasn't listening. "He's not as well-known as Pat Garrett or Wyatt Earp, but they're taken. I went to the library and looked up all the old newspapers where his name appeared. The last one I read mentioned you. That's why you should be the one to write his story. You were with him on his last manhunt."

"I don't follow you. You said you wanted to make a photoplay—a movie—with me, although God knows what you were thinking. I know nothing about movies. Now you want me to write a book, and I'm not sure yet I'm capable of writing the one I'm working on."

"The industry's growing up; that's what they're calling it now, an industry; which is part of the growing up. There's been scandal—drugs and worse. The reason I'm traveling under my real name is I can't be sure a Hollywood character like Buck Jones could book a room in the worst fleabag in town. Tying in with a solid line like publishing is one of the things the business is doing to try and get past all that. Paramount hired a magazine writer to turn the *Forbidden Paradise* script into a book, timing it to hit the stalls the day the movie was released, and it was a smash for Pola Negri. *The Spoilers, The Covered Wagon*: all books, all box office."

He elbowed aside his plate and leaned his weight on his forearms. Rawlings withdrew his, afraid the actor would grab hold of his hands.

"I'll pay you to turn *The Iron Star* into a genuine autobiography. You know the kind of thing, 'I Shot So-and-So;' dump the politics, play up the melodrama. Man, you were *there*! What was it like?"

Rawlings pushed away his plate.

"Dryer than this turkey, when it wasn't raining day and night. The rest of the time it snowed and your blood froze in your veins. Wind all the time, except when it stopped, which was like a gun going off next to your ear, it was that sudden. Then rain or snow again, days of it, and no way to get dry. I had a rash on my privates for a month after I got back to civilization. Do you want that in the book?"

"Maybe not that. But you were with him all that time, practically in his lap. What was *he* like?"

"He claimed to be clairvoyant; not that he knew the word. It did none of us any good in the end, him least of all." Rawlings shook his head. "I'm sorry you wasted a trip, Mr. Jones; but thank you for dinner."

3

CHICAGO WRITES

Just then the waiter came with the bill. Frowning, Jones produced a leather-stitched billfold and counted out singles and change from the coin pocket, lips moving as he calculated the tip. The man left, with another curt bow but no hint of clicking heels.

"I won't try to change your mind here," said the actor. "If you do, I'm at the Railway Arms in Minneapolis."

Starlight rippled on the surface of the Mississippi as they retraced their route. Rawlings said, "I heard you show people in California make fabulous salaries."

"I've heard the same. The press exaggerates, and the studios don't correct it. More people will go see a show if they think Pickford and Keaton make more in a week than they do in a year. They want to see how they earn it."

"It makes sense, in a lunatic way. I only brought it up because there are better places to stay than a railroad hotel."

"I'm on my first contract. I'll need some hits under my belt before I start booking palazzos."

Rawlings shook his head at his reflection in the windscreen. "Did you really expect me to desert my publisher and gamble on an arrangement with no guarantees, for the kind of money you gave our waiter from your Scotch purse? I was surprised he didn't challenge you to a duel."

"I thought"—the actor stopped, breathed, and repeated

it—"I *thought* you might be in the market for an adventure:
like when you traded a desk for a saddle and turned your
back on civilization to chase bandits across the plains. But I
guess that was a long time ago." His voice rasped.

"I told you just how much of an adventure it was. Twenty
years hasn't put a shine on it."

They drove ten blocks with only the sound of the motor
filling the void. Then Jones steered over and switched off the
ignition. Outside, a cicada ran up and down the scale.

"I should have remembered you're a detective," Jones said,
facing his passenger. "I might've taken a different approach;
but I'm no good at wheeling and dealing. The truth is my
face is plastered on every barn and telephone pole from Pitts-
burgh to Pasadena, and I can't get credit for a pack of gum in
Woolworth's. I told you Tom Mix lent me this car; I didn't
tell Tom. He's in Havana, spending what Fox gave him when
he didn't cave on his salary for *Riders*. Since I didn't work as
a lever during the negotiations, I need to cash in on my next
picture or my contract won't be renewed. I'm thirty-seven;
that's too old to go back to busting broncos for the army,
and there isn't even much call for that now that we're getting
on so well with the rest of the world. Of all the rotten luck!"

"You're not making much of a case for your proposition."

"Let me finish. A Boston millionaire named Kennedy
missed out on investing in *The Covered Wagon*, and he's been
kicking his tail ever since. He looked me up; it's important
you understand that, I didn't go to him. I never heard of him
till he bought me lunch in a club in Beverly Hills: oysters
and champagne, pre-war. He liked what I did in *Lazybones*.
He asked me what I was making, and for once in my life I
answered on the level, a hundred and fifty a week. And he
was as honest. I don't guess he's the same with his partners

and competitors, but then maybe I'm not worth the trouble of making up a lie. He said stars take too much off the top, leaving advertising and promotion on the short end, which means shooting craps on their name alone, and Tom Mix doesn't draw 'em in like he used to. 'He's top-heavy,' that's how Kennedy put it: meaning he's gone as high as he can go and you know what's next. But the only way *I* can go is up. He'll stake me to a production, providing he likes the idea; and guess what?"

"You"—Rawlings fished for the word—"*pitched*, that's the word? You pitched *The Iron Star*."

"Sure. Turned out he knew all about the campaign in Missouri. Politics is one of the things he's got a finger in. He said he could've warned St. John against running for office, just like he tried to do with Dewey after Manila. Heroes don't make good legislators, he said, but they sure clean up at the box office." He ducked his head; Rawlings thought the gesture would look better under the ten-gallon hat. "Well, he didn't say 'clean up' or 'box office,' he's lace-curtain Irish; but I followed him okay. Hire somebody to cut all the stumping out of the book, that was his angle: gin up the horses and gunplay and boost interest in the picture before it opens."

"Did you suggest me?"

"No, I kept that close to my chin till I had you in the—till you agreed."

"Why steal—all right, borrow—a car? Why not take the train?"

"Somebody might have seen me at the station. I'm supposed to be shooting close-ups on *The Gentle Cyclone*: Questions would be asked, and Bill Fox isn't exactly open to his contract players straying off the lot in order to consort with the competition."

Rawlings nodded. "I thought it was something like that. You won't stake your job on a pig in a poke, and yet you expect me to stake mine."

Jones turned away and punched the starter. The motor grumbled to life. "I leave Thursday. Tom gets back Monday to start shooting *The Arizona Wildcat*, and I've got to get the horns back on the Caddy and gas it up and give it a wash and wax before he knows it's gone. I'll be suspended when I get back for playing hooky, but I've lived on baloney sandwiches before, with a lot less to look forward to. Keep the book. Maybe some night when you can't sleep you'll open it up and reconsider. Just skip the chapters about Free Silver and tariffs." He let out the clutch.

The next day was Wednesday.

Dr. Titus looked handsome in a hat; unfortunately, Rawlings had seen him wearing one just once, when he arrived late for an examination. He'd survived yellow fever serving in the war with Spain only to have all his hair fall out during treatment. A line like the equator cruelly separated his lean, rectangular face from the scraped bone of his scalp.

He folded his stethoscope and told his patient he could button his shirt. "Pump's running like Man o' War," he said. "Been sneaking onions into your soup?"

Rawlings answered shortly in the negative. Titus thought himself a wit for couching rude accusations in amusing commentary, when in fact he was a lout.

"As you please, but if you don't want me to check you into a ward, you're going to have to take better care of yourself; avoid stimulants of any kind. The minute something begins to excite you, stop."

"You gave me that same advice just before I left the Agency. It's *why* I left, and why I moved here, near the clinic; although six days a week sorting and filing field reports is hardly hunting grizzlies. Since then I've given up liquor, cards, horseback riding, and subtracted all succulents from my diet. I'm thinking of taking up tobacco just to have something left to quit."

"Oh, don't do that." Like all those who regard themselves as droll, Emmanuel Titus was incapable of responding to humor from an outside source. "I'll put it this way: Consider that you were born with a fixed number of heartbeats, and that in order to prolong your existence you must discover some method of slowing them down. Now, that's a highly unscientific theory, and as a physician I'm required not to assign it any weight at all, but in your case the spirit if not the letter holds some wisdom."

"Doctor, you're an ass."

The other chuckled, characteristically mistaking a remark made in dead earnest for a joke. He rose from his stool, unlocked and opened a cabinet, and took out an evil-looking brown bottle stopped with a rubber eyedropper.

"This is new," he said. "It's known to restore regular rhythm during an episode. One or two drops in eight ounces of water, and not more than once in twenty-four hours. It's derived from coal oil. Only a quack would recommend drinking kerosene in quantity."

"You're prescribing poison."

Titus assumed his baggy smile. "If there were a gentler way to say it, I would."

Rawlings accepted the bottle.

* * *

St. Mary's Hospital, home of the Mayo Clinic, was a ten-minute trolley ride from Mrs. Balfour's house. He arrived on the doorstep simultaneously with the postman, who recognized him and separated a long envelope from his handful and gave it to him. It bore a Chicago postmark. The Cyclops eye in the upper left corner seemed to be glaring at him exclusively; which was the intention.

He waited until he was in his room and his hat and coat hung on the tree before slitting it open, using the fifteen-ounce Bowie he kept on the desk for a conversation piece; not that anyone ever dropped by to break the ice.

That sinister eye was repeated at the top of the page above the motto—parodied onstage and in the street, and indisputably part of the Yankee landscape—"We Never Sleep."

Dear Sir:

It has come to the attention of this Agency that you are preparing a book about its activities for the purpose of publication.

It has further come to our attention that you are a former employee of the Agency, and that in compliance with its regulations and bylaws you signed an agreement upon your departure in which you pledged to disclose no details of the Agency's methods, inner operation, or sensitive details of investigations authorized by its management and undertaken by its personnel, deputies, and assignees that were entrusted to your knowledge, on pain of forfeiture of your pension and prosecution for breach of contract; that the document was endorsed by two witnesses and notarized and is legally binding.

We therefore demand that you cease and desist all pursuit

of this project as of the date of receipt of this communication, destroy all notes and records pertaining, and notify this
office of your compliance with this demand. You have until
thirty days of the date of this communication to respond in
the affirmative. Failure to do so will result in a summons
to appear before a magistrate and be prepared to show just
cause as to why you should not be prosecuted for violating
the terms of your agreement.

[signed]
Alver S.P. Fireside, Esq.
Chief Counsel,
Pinkerton's National Detective Agency

He spent an hour at his desk drafting a reply to the letter, and another hour crossing out sentences, substituting
others, and filling the wastebasket with the discards. His
argument, that he had obtained permission to "pursue the
project" from William A. Pinkerton himself, with the un-
derstanding that Rawlings would submit the finished man-
uscript to his office for review; but of course the director
was aware of that, and of Fireside's letter: He'd have insisted
on "reviewing" it before it went out.

He drafted another letter, this one addressed to New York
City, explaining the situation to his publisher, expressing his
regrets, and offering to return the $500 advance—hoping that
the gesture would be magnanimously refused; he'd spent it all
months ago. He stuck it in a pigeonhole, to be revised later.

His hand shook as he replaced his pen in its holder; his
heartbeats were coming so close together they made a continuous hum. He got up, retrieved the brown bottle from
the pocket of his overcoat, added two drops to a tumbler he

filled from the pitcher on the washbasin, and emptied it in one long draught. He went out into the hallway.

The telephone was on the wall. He unhooked the receiver and jiggled the toggle.

"Railway Arms, Minneapolis," he told the operator.

4

DRAGGING THE CISTERN

Railroad hotels had changed since the days when Rawlings traveled at the mercy of the Agency's tight fist.

Jones's accommodations were simple, but the space was clean, with sturdy chairs, a bed that appeared to suit the purpose, and an unexpected luxury: a telephone in the room—the candlestick type, brass, on a table with a marble top. Commuter locals shrieked to a stop within arm's length of the building, and once an express shot past close enough to rattle the panes in the window, interrupting conversation; but the visitor would as soon put up there as in his room in Rochester, had it only the advantage of the Mayo Clinic close by.

The cowboy star had placed a long-distance call to Boston and was waiting for the operator to ring back. Today he looked a little more like his posters, in a blue flannel shirt fastened to the neck with pearl snaps, much-laundered dungarees, and a wide leather belt with a brass buckle. A pair of tooled leather boots on the floor of the open wardrobe bore at least a superficial resemblance to the trail-broken type worn by Irons St. John and most of his posse, twenty years ago and half a continent away. There was no sign of The Hat.

Jones was sitting on the edge of the bed in his stocking feet. He'd pushed aside an open strap suitcase to make room. Inside were shirts, socks, and three stout bottles wrapped in straw; fresh purchases, Rawlings guessed, from across the river. He'd been stocking up for the trip home.

"Kennedy will kick at some of this," he said, pursing his lips over the sheet of notepaper containing the demands Rawlings had written in his clerical hand. "Five hundred cash on signing; he'll cut that in half, but I don't guess you'll lose his respect. You'll never get a piece of the film, I can promise you that. Tom Mix doesn't. Don't think he hasn't tried."

"I'd be giving up more than that if I came in with you. I'm here as a favor, in return for dinner. It took only ten minutes to compose that list on the train. I spent the rest of the trip making notes on my history of Pinkerton's."

He couldn't tell if Jones saw through his bluff. The man was an actor, and presumably in charge of his facial expressions.

"Well, let's wait for the ink to dry on this manifesto before we start burning bridges." He laid the sheet on the nightstand. "I had breakfast, but I wish you'd let me send out for something for you."

"I ate on the train, not knowing what to expect. The last time I was in one of these places the boy held us up for a cartwheel dollar just to fetch a pint of whiskey."

"I thought you were teetotal."

"I am, these days. I just meant twenty years is a long time."

"When you say *us*,—?" Jones let it hang.

"Me, St. John, George American Horse, Bill Edwards, that filthy cur Pierce, and the Menéndezes: all cutthroats except St. John and the Indian." And in a pinch his money would have been on the Indian.

Jones got up to answer the telephone. "Go ahead, operator."

It was a conversation that keenly interested Rawlings, but

the situation called for a show of casual indifference. He rose and went to the window, which looked out on the roof of the station. Beneath the overhang a loafer wearing a straw boater leaned against a post, building a cigarette. The same man had performed the same operation against the same post in Cheyenne and Denver, Laramie and Colorado Springs; only the fashions had changed. Rawlings focused his concentration on him while the exchange behind him rose and fell uncomprehended. His future was being planned across fourteen hundred miles, and he stood watching a stranger manufacturing a smoke.

The *plop* of the earpiece being replaced brought him around.

"He's heard of you," Jones said.

"He has the advantage. I never heard of him."

"He didn't get to be a millionaire at thirty by neglecting his homework. Just since I pitched him he's made himself an expert on that last manhunt. You've got your five hundred, and he'll consider paying a flat fee once the movie starts shooting—if it does. You can't count on anything in this business, except that nobody in it would split the profits with Babe Ruth if he sold them his life story. I couldn't get him to budge on that." He looked at Rawlings. "Are you all right?"

"Of course." He remained standing. He wasn't sure he could make it back to the chair without shaking.

There was some discussion of deadlines, by which time he had control of his voice. "Just how much of the book am I expected to use? I doubt I can salvage fifty pages."

"Use your judgment. Nobody else will be reading it, so who's to know? It wasn't exactly *Ben Hur* the first time." A hammered pewter flask stood on the nightstand. The actor poured two inches of amber fluid into a glass, topped it off with water from a pitcher, and drank.

Rawlings asked if he had another glass.

Fifty pages had been overly optimistic.

Back in his room, he riffled through the rough-trimmed leaves of *The Iron Star,* stopping here and there in search of passages he could reasonably attribute to the man he remembered, not to his ghost collaborator. It was like dragging a cistern for a nugget of gold.

A chapter headed "The Hunt for Hardin" appeared side-by-side with "Nationalizing the Railroads: A Simple Solution." The latter was dry electioneering, and anything to stir the blood in the former was hearsay, if not out-and-out fable, as St. John would have been in Judge Parker's jail in Oklahoma at the time the law was closing in on the Texas mankiller. Rawlings had a clerk's memory for dates.

That, he thought—the bad man in irons, waiting for either a rope or a reprieve—would be a movie he'd part with a dime to see. But he could picture Jones shaking his head, horrified: Kennedy would leave them flat at the suggestion. One didn't need to be an expert to sense that much.

After discarding pre-war politics, stale hyperbole, and material cribbed from dime novels and *Frank Leslie's Illustrated Newspaper,* he was left with a dozen random scenes and a title, which had begun to lose even what appeal it had had. On one page, our hero spoke like Davy Crockett, "palaverin' with the red devils" with a plug in his cheek; on the next he was quoting Shakespeare. Neither extreme suited the man Rawlings had known—well, not *known*; who did, including men who'd served with him for years? But he could hear his voice now, harsh and burring, yet somehow reassuring, like the steady rumble of a ship's engine beneath one's feet: a voice accustomed to shouting orders in open country.

One line alone stood out (was this the nugget?): "In order to run a highwayman to ground, you have to learn to think like him: drink where he drank, eat what he ate, bathe in the same stream, and sleep in the bed he slept in." That at least sounded like St. John; in fact, Rawlings was almost sure he'd heard it from him directly. But there was something wrong with it, a piece torn out. Just what it was continued to gnaw at him after he closed the book.

When it came, he was thinking of something else.

The man Kennedy had agreed, apparently without argument, to pay five hundred dollars to a stranger for what amounted to no more than six weeks of work. Investors from back East didn't become millionaires by acceding to the first demand.

It was the Buckner episode all over again. Rawlings had been ordered to leave his desk behind and take to the field, without explanation and with only one day to prepare. He'd known he was far from the first choice; someone more qualified had suddenly become unavailable and everyone else with experience was either on assignment or beyond reach of a telegram. The Union Pacific was the Agency's most important client; it could not be put off, and so a green clerk had been tapped. Kennedy must be desperate to break into Hollywood.

Either that, or this was all part of some program, engineered in detail before it launched: The invasion by California into his stagnant life, old recollections resurrected from interment, Pinkerton's unexpected withdrawal of permission to publish his history—

But that was absurd. The easterner's influence could not possibly spread that far, and in any case Emmett Force Rawlings wasn't that important; not to anyone, and certainly not to someone accustomed to shooting billiards on the cloth of a continent at seven figures a ball.

Anyway, the Agency answered to presidents only, and not always to them.

He pressed his thumb to his wrist. The course of his thinking wasn't even enough to raise his pulse rate above the usual. That was his barometer, better even than St. John's rheumatism for gauging the weather.

That was when it came, at an oblique angle, while his mind was elsewhere:

In order to run a highwayman to ground, you have to learn to think like him.

It sounded like him, certainly enough. . . .

Yes. Rawlings had heard it more than once during the long stretches of crushing boredom, still a vivid memory twenty years away from the outlaw trail: rocking half-asleep in the saddle, drinking green whiskey cut with some variety of sewage in a fetid saloon where the Buckner gang—brothers Race and Merle, James Blaine Shirley, the gunhand with no hands—had stopped to rest and change horses on their winding way to Mexico (or Canada, or Alaska Territory, or Cuba; all places where they'd been reported by eyewitnesses).

In order to run a highwayman to ground, you have to learn to think like him: drink where he drank, eat what he ate, bathe in the same stream, and sleep in the bed . . .

How had the rest of it gone? And why should he remember it as well as he did?

Because he was trained not as a detective, but as a stenogra-

pher, and habitually wrote down what he couldn't trust himself to get right later.

He dropped the book on the desk, shoved himself away
from it, and went out to find Mrs. Balfour.

5

ANCIENT GLYPHS

The ring the landlady produced from the pocket of her skirt was a brass hoop as big around as a softball, enough to support its clanking half-pound of keys, but Rawlings identified the one he'd asked for without direction. There was only one keyhole in the house big enough to take it. One deft twist and the door was open; like an old married couple, years of contact had worn the wards and tumblers to each other's touch.

Although routine caution had prevented her from surrendering the ring to her tenant, two years' prompt payment of rent and his courtesy in the matters of noise and favors asked had earned him unsupervised access to the treasures in the basement: The pickles were safe. She pocketed the keys and left him on the threshold.

That part of the house wasn't wired for electricity. He carried his borrowed oil lamp down narrow yawning steps, pushing its oblong of light ahead of him through darkness and dry rot. Jars of preserves on shelves gleamed in the reflected illumination.

It was a dugout, with a dirt floor and walls built of irregular stone, originally intended to store roots and provide shelter when Minnesota stood up on its hind legs and howled. He wondered that it didn't seem to do that as often as in the past; had the frontier been settled—literally settled—as thoroughly as a horse broken to the saddle? Was there a place in the book for such musings?

He shook his head. He was getting ahead of himself. What he was looking for may not even be there, or more likely prove to be of no use.

Timber posts supported the floor above. They were as hard as iron and as old as the Norman invasion. He had to stoop to clear the beams that connected them. In the middle of the earthen-smelling gloom, yellow and blue flame glowed between the teeth of the cast iron furnace grate. He used that and his lamp to guide him to the corner where the residents deposited their accumulated goods, ostensibly shielded from dust from the coal bin by a canvas wagon-cover stained black with soot.

The sight exasperated him. He'd removed his coat at the base of the stairs and hung it on a nail, but nothing short of stripping completely would protect his shirt, waistcoat, and trousers from ruin. Resigned, he covered the lower half of his face with his free forearm and twitched off the cover. Coarse granules ballooned up and settled over him from head to foot.

He spent five minutes brushing off the worst of it, along with cobwebs and spider-sacs bunched like grapes, dusted his palms, and regarded his bounty: trunks and train cases, parasols and portmanteaux, rocking chairs, rolled rugs, Christmas wreaths, anonymous cartons and crates, and more filth. No rats, thank God; they'd departed along with the turnips and potatoes. Mrs. Balfour was no cook, and laid no board for her tenants.

Lifting the lamp, he passed it around the assemblage until the light fell on a museum piece: a relic of the days when travelers brought along all their wardrobe for the Grand Tour. It was stenciled in white on crazed black leather:

E. F. RAWLINGS
117 POST STREET
SAN FRANCISCO, CALIF.

Of course it occupied the corner farthest from him. He worked his way toward it, high-stepping over heaps of jetsam—treading on some—and shunted aside a pile so he could scoot the steamer trunk into position. It was three feet wide and four feet high, big enough to contain a small adult; constructed of oxhide on an elmwood frame, nearly indestructible, and stupendously heavy even when empty. It wasn't empty. He set the lamp on a packing case and began his investigation in its light.

The trunk was unlocked; the key, he remembered suddenly, was decorating the necklace of a reservation Arapaho named Split Hoof, if he hadn't drunk himself to death on Jamaica rum. He unlatched and parted the two halves to expose a set of shallow drawers on one side and a rod dangling empty plywood clothes-hangers on the other. A green metal strongbox wallowed on the bottom.

The drawers yielded with a struggle. The first three were stuffed with loose papers and stacks of pocket notebooks bound in peeling leather, each sporting the all-seeing eye, and each filled with pencil notations in the Pittman shorthand that had secured his employment with the Agency after he'd resigned from the Cattleman's Trust Bank in Denver; ironically, one the Buckners had robbed, although that was after he'd left. Dozens of these, meticulously dated by their owner. The loose papers were a motley gleaning of foolscap, stained brown wrap, cigarette cards, and Western Union envelopes; he'd run out of notebooks, but not the mania to record what he'd experienced. All of this had awaited the moment when his research for the history became personal.

Time and graphite were incompatible. Some of the symbols had faded so badly they would take hours to decipher, if at all, like glyphs on clay tablets.

The bottom drawer came free only when he grasped both finger-rings and tugged at it with equal pressure; an odor of dry decay puffed out, along with bits of crumbled pulp. It was stuffed with newspaper cuttings, brown and brittle, dated in pencil—his hand—with the names from the mastheads scribbled in the margins: *The Helena Herald, The Denver Tribune, The Idaho Recorder, The Cheyenne Leader, The Kansas City Times, The Salt Lake Reporter; Miners* by the tramload; a party convention of *Republicans, Democrats,* and *Independents*; Buffalo *News*es, Buffalo *Recorders*, Buffalo *Spectators*, Buffalo *Daily Advertisers*, a herd, spread hundreds of miles apart; some weekly farm journals, a smattering of community broadsides issued whenever there was news enough to report. Some were stuck together, others so fragile they fell to pieces when touched, like cinders; still others were faded blank. Each crumbling scrap had in its time provided a morsel of intelligence sufficient to justify pressing on, deeper and deeper yet into the wild. The hoard of desiccated paper represented labels on the luggage of a traveler with a highly specialized experience of the world.

The strongbox was locked, he'd anticipated that—what was the good of one that wasn't?—and had fished the key from the drawer of the rolltop where he kept odds and ends he couldn't decide whether to hang on to or throw away. He swung up the lid and rooted among the litter of paper bank bands, long since plundered of their greenbacks, loose silver and copper, and blank expense sheets, coming at last to a small bundle. Laying it atop the papers on his lap, he unfurled the roll of yellow sheepskin into an irregular square stained brown, releasing a potent smell, acrid but not unpleasant, like vanilla extract mixed with iodine. A lifetime had passed since he'd inhaled it last, but it was strong enough to send him spinning back to St. Louis, 1906.

The Colt's Thunderer was a double-action revolver, built to ride comfortably in a pocket, but packed a wallop. It could knock a man down at close range, and had. The blued steel glistened. He picked it up, just for the feel of its walnut grip, polished from handling, its heft.

He replaced it, closed the lid, hesitated with the key in his hand, then went ahead and relocked it. Someone might stumble upon the revolver and find it still worked. Apart from that it was no longer relevant, as important as it once had been; and it had been, every bit of that. He'd come for the notes and cuttings.

A crate claiming to contain an accordion from Sears, Roebuck, and Co. (another promising musical career struck down *in utero*) made an acceptable seat. He drew it up, selected an item at random, and went to work. If Irons St. John were going to have anything to do with telling his life's story, this was where it began.

II

IN HIS OWN WORDS

1

EARLY LIFE

I was born in Rockville, Maryland, March 12, 1856, to Thomas and Victoria Venable St. John; their third child and the first to survive infancy. I hardly remember my mother, partly because she died when I was eleven during an outbreak of diphtheria but mostly because she never spoke a word that I can recall, hammered down as she was by the fierce presence of my father, who sold supplies and provisions to the U.S. Naval Academy in Annapolis, diverting such goods as could be concealed from the authorities to Southern interests before martial law was declared.

Thomas I remember well, as I still carry fistulas from his brass belt buckle. They proceeded to ooze some time after he left me to the responsibility of relatives in Illinois. I never saw him after that, though I heard he was hanged by a carpetbagger court when his wartime activities came to light. I was never convinced, and slept with a fish knife in a sheath strung around my neck for a year and a half against his return.

By the time I figured it didn't matter, I was in old Mexico as a guest of President Díaz, who took exception to gringos running guns to revolutionists. See, I'd skedaddled at sixteen to fight for the redistribution of land, and once gunpowder gets into your belly, plain tortillas don't satisfy; but this time I backed the wrong mule. I guess you'd say my family had a close association with hemp, as it was bribery alone that got me out of that adobe cell in Durango while the hammers and saws were busy erecting my stairway to Providence. It wouldn't be my last acquaintance with that variety of departure. Of all the men I played a part in introducing to it I never saw one dangle. It's an allergy I wasn't able to shake. Give me a running battle and a clean shot every time.

Freedom fighting has its diversions—don't the señoritas prefer a rangy wolf in *bandoleros* to a cane cutter, though?—but the days and nights do run together between skirmishes, and you can wake up only so often in a cave in Chihuahua with a rat asleep in your lap before it pales on you, so I'd taken French leave to go north and chase payroll trains in New Mexico and Arizona. See, it was *mestizo* bandits bought me free of that noose, and like they say, it's the company you keep.

I played cards through the bars for a month after a disagreement with the Texas & Pacific Railroad, but they cut me loose when a postal clerk couldn't place my face because of his cracked skull—he said. You'd think Washington City would employ someone to smell a man's breath before putting him in charge of a mail car. None of us ever laid so much as a hand on him, much less a pistol butt.

Understand, I'm not boasting of my wandering and dissolute youth. I had a rash I couldn't scratch ever since tenderhearted old Tom St. John unloaded me on his cousins to work off my bed and board in the city stockyards; I'm told I can still hold a grudge till it sprouts treasury bills, but if that's so, Old Man Ike's no fit match for *El Negrito Corazón*—that's what they called me south of the border, Little Black Heart. I soured a long time on that vine. Well, I owe my redemption to a Cajun bushranger nobody'd ever have heard of if it wasn't me that shot him.

Back when I first got famous, *Frank Leslie's Illustrated Newspaper* sent a scribbler to get my story. If I knew my answer to his first question would show up as much as it did I might have put more time into selecting my words. He wanted to know my winning philosophy for hunting men. What I said was this:

"In order to run a highwayman to ground, you have to learn to think like him: drink where he drank, eat what he ate, bathe in the same stream, and sleep in the bed he slept in; with the same whore, if possible. One time, Jack LeFever and I shared the same dose of clap."

I shouldn't have to tell you that last part never went to press, for the benefit of the children and unmarried women who might see the periodical laying about and pick it up out of curiosity; but these things will get out. Although I can't swear to it, that little parcel of wisdom may have had something to do with why I'm not sitting in the Congress. I wouldn't have said it except the interview took place in a private booth in the sampling room of the Acropolis Hotel in Bismarck, where the whiskey came in the original bottles. The curtains were thick, but voices carry.

Anyhow I'm wedded to it, same as Honest Abe and them rails he never split but one, for the press in Springfield when he was pleading for the railroad. Just last year, in Joplin for a debate, I had a lady come up to me at a roast-beef dinner to tell me she was there in Casper the day I rode in with Jack's carcass slung across a pack horse; she even had the color, sorrel, and as she expressed it, I drew rein right there in the middle of First Street to lean down from the saddle and kiss her square on the lips, just on account of she was standing there looking pretty. She was fourteen at the time, she said, and it ruined her reputation. But Jack drew his last dishonest breath in Miami in the Indian Territory in 'seventy-six, and she was sixty if she was a day when she told me that story, so I guess it's so what they say, that scandal ages you. I never was in Casper so far as I recall, and if I come in with a dead man in my traps I sure would. You see how far a little moonshine can spread without much of a downhill start. That's history for you.

1926

Oral history ignores chronology. A man shares details of his past adventures in the order they come to him. To contrive the illusion of a memoir intended for publication, Rawlings had to slog through notes that might include a reminder to pick up side meat and tobacco at the next outpost of civilization as well as a revealing confession from St. John's "wandering and dissolute youth;" mark the reference, and insert it in its proper place. The process was like a game of dominoes, minus the entertainment.

It had taken an hour to find the first mention of Jack Le-Fever and the rest of the quotation that had been taunting him. By then the flame in the lamp was stuttering, the glass chimney smudged black from turning up the wick; a self-defeating measure, as it made the light feebler still.

The ragged nature of his penciled hand when he came to the old marshal's advice to manhunters put him back on the scene where he'd first heard it. It was possible, by factoring in his shorthand speed at the time, to count the places where the joints in the tracks had spoiled his symbols and calculate the rate at which they were traveling.

They'd been swaying over a set of rails warped beyond

the common, in a private coach provided by the Southern Pacific in cooperation with the governor's office in Wyoming, which was financing the expedition from the state treasury. Rosewood marquetry paneled the walls, a stained-glass fixture broke the light into candy colors, and the carpet beneath their feet had once hung on the wall of a villa in Venice; the party trod upon the faces of gods, heroes, and three-headed dogs. Green velvet curtains swaddled a four-poster bed from the Second Empire. The supervisor of the Wichita-to-Denver route had told them Jay Gould himself had slept in it, although he couldn't confirm whether he'd shared it with any particular whore.

Irons St. John—"Ike" to his intimates, of which George American Horse had been the only one present—"Cap'n" to the rest—sat legs crossed in a horsehair chair, one hand holding coppery liquid in a leaded glass and the other a Simón Bolívar cigar, between the pads of his thumb and forefinger, the same way he clutched a cigarette. The smoke was as thick as chowder. He was a big man for his profession; in Rawlings' limited experience, peace officers ran short and wiry and blended easily into crowds; but this one's frame, broad and raw-boned but taking on flesh, required the full support of the tall claybank stud riding in the stock car. His horse-collar moustache was shot with gray and his skin burned terra-cotta, ending in a swath of white where it met the sweatband of his hat when he wore it; and he seldom didn't.

Buck Jones would not appear in public dressed as St. John; the people who bought tickets to see the cowboy star perform would never accept him in a coarse pullover sweater of un-dyed wool, trousers striped like ticking, and plain square-toed boots the color of sand. The drab sweater didn't suit him; it made his face look florid and his face made the wool look like putty. The air about him swam with camphor and stale cedar.

It was a moment of repose; and rare as they were, brief acquaintance had already taught the Pinkerton to brace himself for a lecture on the science of trailing fugitives.

"Wild Bill" Edwards—the long-distance assassin—paused to breathe on the lenses of his spectacles, then resumed polishing them with a handkerchief embroidered with initials he wasn't using at present. "We heard that story, Cap'n: back in St. Louis, and again in Jeff City."

"And you will again, Bill, till I know it took hold. George, here, knows what I'm talking about. Injuns only know what their granddaddies learnt the hard way from spinning the same old yarns till you can't stand the sound of 'em."

"We still have to learn them even then," said the Crow. "You have to take a squat in the saw grass yourself to remember not to do it again."

George American Horse remained an anomaly. He was the first full-blooded Indian Rawlings had seen outside a picture book. Small pox had left its brand on his round face, time and fatty reservation food on his waistline, and he tucked his plaits up inside a shapeless hat with pheasant feathers in the band. He wore a rusty black tailcoat over his naked chest and corduroy breeches reinforced with buckskin and stuffed into the tops of stovepipe boots. He'd come in answer to St. John's wire from the shambles of his campaign headquarters in St. Louis, directly from a season with a seedy Wild West show, bringing Edwards along. Edwards, the sharpshooter, had earned his keep riding around in circles and potting at glass balls while George "wrassled" the show's star in a barbarous costume for the entertainment of audiences, losing once a day and twice on Saturdays.

The Pinkerton hadn't made up his mind how much of this toadying to the posse chief was genuine. It carried a note of amused tolerance that was a sign of either affection or derision; possibly a combination of both. These men had ridden together, fed from the same plate, and shared each other's blankets since before the frontier closed. Rawlings was an outsider and always would be no matter how much time he spent in their company. There was just too much ground lost.

So he had nothing to lose by calling the iron marshal to account.

"Wasn't it killing LeFever that got you measured for a noose in Fort Smith?"

2

FORT SMITH

I've gone and uncorked the LeFever business, which I wasn't intending to do till you got to know me better, but it's out now and I don't want to go back and risk losing my bearings and stray wide of the path.

Jack was a born salesman. Gold bricks were his specialty, but in a pinch he sold town lots, put in orders for mining equipment (taking deposits up front), peddled lightning rods and truck like that, and when four customers showed up to claim ownership of the same lot, or Monkey Ward pled ignorance of any representative in its employ named LeFever, or the lightning rod turned out to be made of spruce and therefore useless, he would fall back on the staples, selling gold bricks and such. He had a gift for reading the clientele, and if they'd got wind that his merchandise was not as advertised he knew it, and adjusted his approach accordingly. I could've used him last November.

However, for every natural advantage God gives to His offspring, there is a deficiency, and Jack's was that as good as he was at interpreting the expression on a man's face, he couldn't always read the man, especially if that man was cut from similar cloth. He'd fell into the notion that he was the only fox in any chicken coop he walked into.

I'd just arrived in Miami, in the old Indian Nations, and having shook loose finally of a party of bad sports in Baxter Springs, I was in a ragged state, which I allow made me look a good prospect. Jack was a skinny jasper who appeared taller than he was on account of he displaced so little from side to side; his clothes draped his external construction like a picture in a mail-order catalogue, not at all like they did for the rest of us when we tried them on, and he wore one of those little sets of whiskers that get stuck under your fingernail. He could pass for a floorwalker or a prince of Egypt. All of which had me watching him out of the tail of my eye while I rubbed down the chestnut mare I was riding at the time, using the community burlap sack.

You can't always judge a man by how he's dressed. Anyone can lay hold of a decent suit of clothes, but a good mount is another story. He was combing the tail of a roan gelding so old and scraggy you couldn't tell where the burrs left off and the horse began. I doubt it even remembered what a filly used to be for. Right away I knew Jack wasn't much farther ahead of a disenchanted customer than I'd been of that posse.

But I wasn't the only one studying his neighbor. Pretty soon he put down his curry and flipped up the fender to get to what was too good a saddlebag for the animal carrying it.

What he took out was a small bundle wrapped in blue cloth, which unwound was a narrow wood box like the kind faro dealers use to dispense cards, varnished and painted all over with stars and planets. There was a little cutout in the top so you could see right down to the bottom and it was empty. Seeing he had my attention, he slid a flat oilskin wallet from the town suit under his duster, dealt himself a rectangle of rag paper, put back the wallet, and laid the paper inside the box. Then he shunted a little wood panel that was built inside forward and back, and there in the bottom was a crisp new two-dollar bank-note with a hairy face engraved on it.

"You impress me, sir, as a man who might welcome a stroke of good fortune," says he; "certainly nothing to arouse shame in these times of panic and economic depression. I am prepared to offer you, in addition to this marvel of modern invention, exclusive rights to distribute it throughout these United States and the Dominion of Canada, for the slender sum of five dollars American; including, as a token of brotherhood, the treasury note whose manufacture I have just demonstrated: an immediate forty-percent return on your investment."

Of course I brought up the obvious, but he barged in before I finished.

"Naturally, I could go on producing notes for my own use, so you're properly skeptical of my motivation in parting with this engineering masterpiece for any amount. But what would I be if, set for a lifetime as it has made me, I were to hoard it to myself and withhold it from my fellow traveler? Worse than Herod! Initially I considered letting it go for free gratis, but then it occurred to me that man is a suspicious creature, who places upon an item of merchandise the same value as does the vendor, and so declines to participate; and so the five dollars, you see, is purely symbolic.

"Here, take it and try it for yourself; remove the demonstration note first and pocket it. I'll contribute the raw paper, which is obtainable from any well-stocked stationer's for pennies. I caution you against using plain pulp, as it lacks the proper texture, which may incite suspicion of counterfeit and also jam the mechanism or even damage it."

I grinned at him without taking it. "Mister," I said, "you should run for public office. A man of your parts could walk across the Potomac."

He cocked one eyebrow, which takes skill; I never could manage it myself.

"I don't collect your meaning, sir. Are you questioning the worth of my product?"

"Not a bit of it. It's a handsome piece of trick cabinetry, but it don't bear comparison to the man holding it. I'd pay to watch you sell oil to a sardine."

His face went black and his easy smile shrank to a pucker. "You saying I'm a liar?"

See, he'd stopped diagramming his sentences. I hadn't come across that particular tell before, but any change is worth paying attention to when you call a man out for what he is. I seen he was unarmed, which is what made me so bold, but I hadn't overlooked the big Walker Colt in his saddle scabbard, and when he twisted that direction I jerked the sporting piece from the boot behind my chestnut's cantle and put a wad of double-ought buck in his left kidney, close enough to set his duster on fire. My ears rang like a fire bell.

He didn't die straight off. They don't always, unless it's in the heart or the brain and sometimes the liver, and even then they're like to twitch, so if you're the excitable type you might waste lead defending yourself unnecessarily. But I don't like to see a fellow flop around, even if he did try to fleece me out of my last five dollars, so I gave him the other barrel. He was down on the ground already, and I had to crab-walk around his horse, which was rearing and looking for a place to plant a hoof after its master slid down its flank stinking of blood and shit, to get a clear shot. I'm happy to report my mare held her ground. I'd won her in a game of high-five off a sergeant discharged from the Comanche wars.

Two charges from a ten-gauge raised about as much fuss in the Nations as a possum fart. Nobody shot at me or gave me so much as a sour look all the way back to the rooming house where I bought a second-floor back with Jack's two dollars, pocketing the change. It was a perfectly good note that he'd put in the false bottom of the box for seed; I'd rescued it, leaving the marvel of modern invention on the ground where he'd dropped it when he went for the horse pistol. I doubted it would bring me any better luck than it had him.

I might as well have hung onto it, though, for all the good it did me when a deputy U.S. marshal kicked open my door and threw down on me with a Russian .44.

He couldn't have timed it better. I was sitting on the edge of a cornshuck mattress in my long-handles and the dirt of three states, with nothing to throw at him but the boot in my hand, and I was never so good at pitching horseshoes I'd bet my roll on it against four-tenths of an ounce of lead. His name was Ames.

We didn't set off right away. He chained me to a chest of drawers while he went out and scoured the town for names of witnesses who'd seen Jack and me go into the stables five minutes apart and only me come out, having heard two blasts inside. That was a surprise. I'd always heard a man's hide didn't count for much in that territory, and I can't say but it wasn't the first time I was arrested by a man who knew his letters. It seemed like a lot of trouble to go through for a tinhorn from Louisiana.

I wasn't the first to cross into Arkansas in shackles, though you'd think I was from the attention we attracted in Fort Smith. There wasn't much in that clutch of military blockhouses to compete with the spectacle peculiar to Fort Smith. It had to do with an impressive piece of mortise-and-tenon construction, twenty feet long and half a story high with an I-beam twelve inches thick running across the top, whitewashed top to bottom. It occupied a stockade behind a stone building they called the commissary and was clearly visible through the gate, which from the look of it had hung open since the last trooper left the garrison five or six years before I saw it. Not much had been accomplished in the way of gentrification since, on the sow's-ear principle.

Ames caught me looking, and wrenched the jerkline that ran from his saddle horn to my manacles; he valued his breath at twenty dollars a word and so saved money that way.

"It will hold your likes right enough if that's what concerns you; and eleven more to boot. The Judge admires to save 'em up."

I was impressed. I'd thought I was an expert on gallows science, having seen more than my portion closer up than I cared. They were all made of green wood, built just for the occasion and then taken down the next day, like a Christmas tree once it's fulfilled its obligation; such a sight didn't make a welcoming first impression for the immigrants the town hoped to settle there. Not so the scaffold in Fort Smith: You might say the swift and steady export of condemned souls was its chief source of commerce. The saloons, hotels, and boarding houses swoll up every time a date was set; and when there were two or more in the party you couldn't hire a tree limb inside spyglass range for less than ten dollars gold, though you might consider a group rate on a hot-air balloon. They called the attraction Parker's washline.

3

THE JUDGE

We always called him Old Thunder, but I think now that was only half fair. Oh, when the gallery got rowdy that gavel rung out like a pistol shot sure enough, and his voice shook dust and dead spiders from the ceiling beams when he called the room to order, but if you believe his obituary in *The Fort Smith Elevator* he was only thirty-nine when I first made his acquaintance. I'm given to understand I've a son close to that age; he's a church deacon, so you can accept that or not, as you please.

But in the two years that Isaac Charles Parker had sat on the federal bench, the weight of his responsibilities had struck his head and whiskers with white, and he'd made enough mortal enemies to satisfy a man twice his age. He had the last word over the Western District of Arkansas and all of the Indian Nations, a piece of country about the size of Austria, with a population that would make the House of Hapsburg turn its whiskers to the wall: One man, charged with the protection of the Cherokee, Creek, Choctaw, Chickasaw, and Osage tribes, each with its own local government and police force; which made it ripe pickings for every blackleg north of the Brazos with a price on his scalp. You could hold up a pack train in the Creek, cross over into the Cherokee, and blow in a bank at your leisure, on account of the only authority with jurisdiction in both places was two hundred miles away in Fort Smith. In those days it was like God had picked up the continent and tipped it to the left and all the men and women with a soul managed to hang on tight.

That was before Parker. He'd been in residence just over a week, having traveled by steamboat down the Arkansas from Missouri, when he sentenced eight men to the rope bang off. Six answered the summons, one having been commuted to life in prison by order of the President and the other shot trying to break jail. Five thousand spectators watched the rest shoot through the trap, snapping their necks like a bolt from the sky. "Six Men Jerked to Eternity in a Second!" went one of the headlines back East; they're poets there.

The carcasses weren't cold in the ground when Parker sent invitations to peace officers across the country to keep the gallows in trim. Royal Ames was one. He was a half-breed: Osage and Negro, which wasn't unusual there, though it was most other places. He was an odd-looking cuss, assembled from whatever parts had been laying around at the time; his head was too big for his neck and his arms were short, but he didn't need much room to break your jaw with one of his fists, which when he stuck them in his pockets looked like he was smuggling hogmeat. I consider him the best friend I ever had, that arrest notwithstanding. I cried like a baby when Dick Spanish, that piece of lizard shit, killed him from bushwhack in Pheasant's Bluff in '86. Spanish's own dog gave evidence against him.

Just as one point in Ames's favor, he took my arm on the stairs to the basement in the brick courthouse so I wouldn't fall in the dark. That may not sound like much—maybe you'd say he just didn't want me breaking my neck on that steep grade and cheating the hangman—but there were mar-shals that let gravity do their work for them, and that floor at the bottom didn't give.

There wasn't a cent of taxpayers' money wasted on the old Fort Smith jail. A stone wall ran slap down the middle, sep-arating it into two cells fifty-five feet long by twenty-nine wide (I paced it off enough times to be sure), with nothing but slimy bedrock to sit on, a bucket in the chimney base for necessary purposes, and a kerosene barrel cut in half to squat in and scrub yourself with cold water and yellow soap on bath day. That was how we kept the calendar down there, by counting baths: one every ten days, three to a month. We never did work out a system to know whether it was day or night, windows being a fiscal irresponsibility on the books. In the twenty-one years Parker was in charge, the federal budget never once went into the red.

I won't mention the stench in that cellar, except to say I spent the winter of '75 in Dakota skinning wolves for the bounty, which makes me an expert on the subject.

Four baths into my stay, a turnkey came down with a lan-tern and called my name. He had a harelip, and he had to repeat it, which I guess annoyed him, because he poked me in the back with his stick all the time I dragged my leg irons up that steep flight of stairs.

At the top was a dim quiet hallway ending in a black oak door. He took his stick out of my kidneys to rap on it, opened it and shoved me inside without waiting for an answer.

"Prisoner St. John, Your Honor."

I couldn't see who he was talking to at first. That room had a window looking out on the old parade ground, and I hadn't seen the sun in more than a month. All I could make out was a purple blob in a swirl of green and orange. Gradually my eyes remembered what they're for and filled in the rest; which wasn't much more of a treat. I don't suppose it ever is when you get your first glimpse of the Angel of Death.

"Remove his shackles."

The guard's key grated; oil was another commodity that bare-bones layout scraped by without, probably because the man whose job it was to carry out the will of the court with his bare hands needed it to lubricate the hemp. You never saw a man who struck you as more suitable for his work than George Maledon; but I'm getting ahead of myself again.

More money yet had been saved on the furniture in that room: a big plain desk, two or three stick chairs, a rag rug, and a kind of carousel stocked with books with leather covers. The man who went with the desk had white in his hair and chin whiskers like I said before and wore his coat, vest, and cravat like everyday overalls and not something you put on once a year to see someone hitched or buried. He had thick eyelids that he seemed to have trouble holding up; but that was a trick I knew from poker and would see in practice later. Lawyers that fell for it didn't last long in his court.

He said that'd be all and the guard left. He had a low even voice without any bark on it, but that too was just for the rubes. He asked me if I knew who he was. I said he was Parker. I'd seen his picture once in a whorehouse in the Cherokee Outlet. There wasn't any white in it then. It had six bulletholes in it.

"Only six? It must not have been up there long."

Someone snorted; a red-faced jasper standing stoop-shouldered by the window stuffing a pipe. I hadn't paid him any mind, thinking he was on hand to discuss fiduciary matters relating to the court and nothing to do with me. He looked like a bank president, with an elk's tooth on his watch chain, a shiny bald head, and a gray thatch that started just under his eyes and grew down far enough you wondered why he'd bother with a cravat; but from the rest of him it was a safe bet he did, and tied all proper.

Parker saw where I was looking. "Mr. Upham is United States Marshal for this district. And you are Irons St. John: A good likeness of you hangs in the telegraph office in Little Rock. You were tried last year in Austin for robbing the Texas and Pacific Railroad."

That was a surprise. I'd been led to believe no news ever approached the Nations from any direction. I told him I'd been turned loose by a jury.

"The prosecution was pathetic. I sent for a transcript; that's the reason you were kept waiting. There's no question about the verdict this time. Deputy Ames spoke with witnesses who swore you killed a man in cold blood. You shot him in the back."

"I couldn't wait for him to turn around once he had that Colt in his hand."

Parker rested his forearms on the desk. I would see him do that a dozen times on the bench and it always meant the same thing.

"There is one penalty, and only one, for willful murder under the law, and no appeal between this district and the President; some say almighty God, but I don't subscribe to blasphemy. How old are you?"

I had to figure it up, like bath days. Nobody ever baked me a cake.

He looked sad; but then he always did except when his temper was tested. "I cannot think of a greater tragedy than to die at twenty."

"Ain't that up to the jury?"

"This isn't Texas. The jury will continue to discharge its duty as it has since I accepted this assignment. However."

He cleared his throat, and I braced myself for the thunder, but still it didn't come. "There are special circumstances in this case, which I may or may not rule pertinent according to my lights. It seems LeFever didn't stop at selling worthless goods to gullible strangers. He broke jail in Nebraska, where he was awaiting execution for the rape and murder of a storekeeper's wife. Had you not met, he would have been apprehended and held for extradition to Omaha to hang. It's why Deputy Ames was keeping such a close eye on him."

"I wondered how he happened on me so soon."

"Had you acted one minute later he'd have arrested you on the spot." He shuffled the papers on his desk. "Mark you, the decision I'm considering should not be interpreted as license for just anyone to run out and do the law's work. We've had enough of that in this territory under my predecessors. But such facts have been known to sway jurors."

There was nothing for it but to wait for him to spit out whatever cud he was chewing. I learned a lot of dressy words sitting in Parker's gallery, but I never got his handle on them or I'd be sitting behind a desk of my own right now in Washington instead of getting my bones shook loose aboard this train. Some things you have to be born with.

"Last year," he said, "the Congress granted this court criminal jurisdiction over seventy-four thousand square miles of wilderness, and authorized the appointment of a mere two hundred deputy marshals to patrol it. The job doesn't attract gentlemen. Some of them, I suspect, are scarcely better than the animals they hunt; I don't ask for details, so I don't have to explain myself to Washington. Now it's a risk I have to take."

I was just beginning to get the idea; I was slow in those days. I looked at Upham. "Can he do that?"

He snorted again. He was busy puffing life into his pipe. "Till the Congress says stop, and it hasn't yet."

"From what I heard it ain't much of a pardon."

"I make no promise it will be anything else." Parker flattened his palms on the desk. "The star or the rope, St. John; I won't give you the choice again."

"What's it pay?"

"We'll have the guard back in."

I gave him my answer then. Who knew he was so touchy?

1926

When Rawlings groped his way back up from Mrs. Balfour's basement, only a single light glowed in the foyer: an oil lamp with a painted glass globe. The landlady, who believed electric lights left on overnight could short out and start a fire, had retired. He exchanged his smudged and spent lamp for the one on the table and climbed to his room. His muscles were stiff from sitting hunched over for hours on a packing crate. For the first time he felt something like sympathy for St. John: returned to the saddle at the age of fifty just when it seemed he'd left it for a padded seat in the Capitol Building.

Back at his desk he emptied his pockets of his old notebooks and spread them out on the blotter. Their covers and page-corners curled brown in the illumination of the electric bulb and they gave off a stale odor like old wallpaper. He measured out two drops of the physic his doctor had prescribed into a glass of water, drank it, and resumed reading where he'd left off.

✳   ✳   ✳

When Rawlings brought up Fort Smith, the old lawman's face broke into scores of creases; not necessarily a sign of amusement. Either nothing of his real nature showed on the outside or it all did, all at once. It was like looking at a painting by one of the Impressionists and not knowing whether to stand close or at a distance.

"That was a misunderstanding. Say what you like about the Judge, he was reasonable for a fire-breathing Methodist."

Midian Pierce, the wild card in the old marshal's deck, never participated in the banter. As the train carrying the posse rattled on, the self-professed Sunday school teacher sat on a stiff-backed chair (the closest thing in the private coach to a wooden pew), lips moving over his travel-stained Bible. St. John had introduced him as a remorseless killer; an unpleasant but essential asset in a manhunt, but no one to swap stories with. Rawlings had disliked him on sight, and not just because of what he'd been told. There was something indescribably foul about him, in spite of the pale handsome wax-figure face and clerical dress, Puritan black from the flat crown of his hat to the caps of his shoes. Murder seemed to be the least of his sins.

He interrupted his ecclesiastical studies only to tend his weapons, a barrel-heavy .36 Navy conversion and a bizarre derringer the size and shape of a dollar coin with a two-inch barrel and a squeeze trigger, designed to fit in a man's palm. He dismantled, cleaned, and oiled them from a kit in a slim eelskin case with all the fussy attention to detail of a housewife polishing the good silver. Clearly his fingers had performed the duty so many times his mind was no longer involved: And each time another man dead.

How had Parker described the type? Rawlings flipped back several pages: men "scarcely better than the animals they hunt."

For himself, Rawlings had no illusions about the company's attitude toward him. The Agency had outfitted him with a preposterous past: he was a champion marksman (based on a few practice sessions on the range in Chicago), a veteran field operative based in Cheyenne (a place he had yet to see), and had even killed a man in Mexico (he'd knocked over a pyramid of wooden pins with a ball while on holiday in Tijuana). All this was engineered to manufacture confidence in a stranger, but he sensed a strain of burlesque in St. John's tone when he repeated it to the others. That may have been the Pinkerton's imagination, fueled by embarrassment, but the effect was the same. He was saddled with expectations he'd be obliged to meet.

They were bound for Denver to interview witnesses to a bank robbery in which the Buckners were identified, but when they stopped for water a boy in a bicycle messenger's uniform boarded with a wire that changed their plans. His Adam's apple bobbed twice at the Indian who opened the door. George American Horse grinned and placed a ten-cent piece in the boy's palm. "Boo!"

The messenger was gone so quickly the car jumped back up on its bogies.

"Shame on you, George." St. John took the yellow envelope from him and opened it. "His first grandson will piss his pants every time he walks past a cigar store." He hooked on his spectacles and read. "From Pinkerton's headquarters in San Francisco. A party of U.S. marshals stuck up a train at Elephant Crossing yesterday. Had badges and everything; can't argue with that. Ever hear of the place?"

"Jerkwater on the run from Wichita," Bill Edwards said. "Two tarpaper shacks, the tower, and a shithouse: Quiet spot to run a gold shipment through. I'd consider it myself if I wasn't abstemious these days."

"I like these Buckners; never try the same dodge twice."

"Are we sure it's them?" said Rawlings.

"In Denver they posed as journalists, asking questions about bank security. Folks this talented ought to black their faces and play the banjo." He put away his glasses. "This one's fresh on the vine. Mr. Rawlings, will you fetch the conductor, tell him we're stopping at Elephant Crossing?"

But they made another unscheduled stop, to pick up a pair of mixed-blood Yaquis who flagged them down to offer their services. The Menéndezes—if that was their name—claimed to have ridden with a cattle rustler from Zacatecas who had recently sworn opposition to President Díaz; but the *Federales* had turned up the heat and the reformed cow thief had ordered the band to disperse until the wind blew the other direction. They kept their El Tigre Winchesters in good condition, and since St. John retained a soft spot for revolutionists he'd agreed to recruit them on a probationary basis. Thereafter they were referred to as the Menéndez brothers, although there was no family resemblance. Paco was gaunt, with lank black moustaches and identical scars on both cheeks, Diego fifteen years older and built like a whiskey barrel on bow legs. The marshal's Spanish was rusty and his Indian worse, so no one was sure as to the nature of their relationship.

They slowed again coming up on Cheyenne Wells.

Edwards groaned. "Next time let's take the express. These milk runs get on my nerves."

It was a photographer this time, bearing a letter from the

Governor of Wyoming, directing the party to pose for a picture commemorating the manhunt.

George said, "I thought the election was over."

"It is," said St. John. "But that's just the beginning. He can't make an appointment without the state legislature, and they aren't just sure he don't hold with crime. I never knew how law-abiding I was till I got into politics."

The group arranged itself on the station platform with the locomotive in the background, the Menéndezes each on one knee in front leaning on their carbines, George American Horse and Bill Edwards seated cross-legged between, and the marshal, Rawlings, and Pierce standing in back: Seven somber faces squinting against the sun, soon to be a fixture on front pages and the walls of saloons and barbershops across the country.

When the photographer and his assistant had left carrying the tripod camera and trunkful of glass plates, Rawlings approached St. John, standing under the station canopy in his sheepskin coat. It was old, and the hem had turned up at the back so that the fleece lining showed. His breath mingled with the smoke from his cigar, hanging under the roof like Spanish moss. It was still November, but there was snow piled up on both sides of the tracks.

"You look lost, son. It's lonesome country."

"It's not the country. I seem to be the only one here without a criminal record."

"That's untrue. George has yet to break a statute I heard of, and Bill's never been known by that name in any jailhouse roll. I can't speak for the Mexicans. If they give us trouble we can always shoot them."

"It isn't a thing to joke about."

"I don't disagree."

"It's Pierce who concerns me. He needs to be on a leash."

St. John nodded. He crushed out his cigar against the post and put the stub in a pocket.

"He does for a fact. But when he needs it most it's got nothing to do with killing."

4

I HUNT A WOMAN

You'd be right to ask, considering what I told you of my adventure with Jack LeFever, how he came to share a reputation with famous marauders like Jesse James, Billy Bonney, and my old pards the Dalton boys, whereas he was more likely to take pleasure in the company of a Philadelphia thimble-rigger. That's partly my fault, and partly Judge Parker's; and it all started because of a woman. Don't everything, though?

Clara Hornbeck operated a house of infamy in the unassigned lands between the Creek and Chickasaw, in what's now Shawnee but back then consisted of a store that sold plows and beef jerky, a stock barn where auctions took place, and some shacks; it looked like it'd washed up against the side of the hill when the Cimmaron overflowed its banks. You could ride across it in thirty seconds if you didn't get hung up on clotheslines. Clara's place was more substantial than its neighbors, clapboard built like a sleeper car with a hall down the middle, rooms on both sides, and a fresh coat of whitewash every spring. She ran some comely half-breeds, high yellows, and the occasional treat of a Chinese girl working her way from San Francisco to St. Louis; but our chief interest in her was the lean-to out back she rented to runaway wives and male transients who'd come west for their health; those last were expected to pay up on time and

lay off raiding within three days' ride as a condition of their
stay.

Bob Squire was Clara's favorite; the only road-agent she'd
turn out a woman in need in order to make room for. Some
said they'd enjoyed a common-law relationship in Kentucky,
others that they were coupled legal and proper in Columbus,
Ohio, where Bob was born. Personally I think the whole
story of their romance took place right there in that house. I
had opportunity to observe them together when whatever he
was wanted for at the time didn't fall under federal attention
or upset the Judge's standards of civilized behavior, meaning
murder or female outrage. They were tight as cordwood.

Bob robbed banks and trains, but no one ever saw him
discharge his weapon directly at another soul. In fact, he'd
once stepped between a slow clerk and a high-strung partner
when it looked like the clerk might take a slug in the liver.
(That made the culprit Jim Proudfoot, he being partial to
that remedy.) Bob was a man of character, which I suppose
is what attracted Clara in the first place, because he wasn't
much to look at with his jug ears and stingy chin. She didn't
entertain quality folk often.

Anybody could've told her that her arrangement with fugitives couldn't stay secret. Folks talk, and Fort Smith didn't
exactly stop its ears. Mind, we didn't bang on her door every
time a whiskey smuggler or a dollar-bill-splitter went un-
derground in her neighborhood; we had bigger fish to fry,
and hers was a handy place to drop a line. It was a sight more
pleasant than working, beating the brush and bribing infor-
mants with confiscated liquor. So when an officer with the
Cherokee Lighthorse Police dropped in one day hoping to
overhear some gossip and was told Miss Hornbeck wasn't in
and no one knew when she would be, he pricked up his ears.

He got the same answer the next three visits, and when on the fourth no one came to the door, he kicked it in and found the place empty; not so much as a cottonmouth in residence, the lean-to included. No mystery as to why: Clara was the only one who knew how to keep the books. Anyway, he informed the marshals.

Over the next month, we tracked down four of the girls employed in similar establishments, and Milward, the three-hundred-pound Negro who kept order in the house, quarrying limestone in Eufaula; but none of them could or would offer a suggestion as to where Clara went, only that she went sometime late on the night of the harvest moon, because she wasn't there next morning.

Right around that same time, the Merchant's Bank in Hutchinson, Kansas, had surrendered twenty thousand in cash and securities to four men in grainsack masks, one of which answered Bob Squire's general description as to height, build, and gait due to one foot that turned inside, from an old busted leg that never knit straight. The odds were more than even he'd broke trail straight to Clara's, according to his habit and also her disappearance less than a week after the robbery. That windfall was his best ever, and they weren't likely to find a better retirement stake. All that fresh fruit hanging outside Parker's window could only mean the lawless days on the border were playing out.

Royal Ames, who you'll recall was my first acquaintance with the law in the Nations, was part bloodhound and smarter than Deadeye Dick. He figured out that turning over every rock in the territory looking for a veteran thief like Bob was a waste of manpower, and suggested we look for Clara instead, as Bob was sure to be close by. Her fair skin and red hair just naturally drew attention to her there in squaw country, and anyway no well-set-up woman could escape notice for long, regardless of what disguise she attempted. Nor was either of them likely to quit a place they knew and where they could count on friends to give them cover; also they'd be traveling in high style thanks to that bank in Kansas—otherwise why bother?—and the prairie pirates in Texas and Mexico couldn't be expected to observe professional courtesy.

It was natural to suppose the pair would drift west, to put distance between them and Parker's court, but Bob was too slippery to swim with the current, so we split off from the other marshals to try the Choctaw along the eastern border. Camping on the Arkansas the first night, I asked Ames why he'd picked me to partner with instead of a man with more experience on his side of the badge—and less on the other.

He let that steep a minute, then said, "That there's the reason," and turned over and went to sleep.

Well, he wasn't a man to spin words like jute, and I was green. It took me years to winnow it out; that we were recent acquaintances and blank slates, so to speak. All we knew about each other was he didn't throw me downstairs when that would have been convenient, and I only shot a man because he was thin-skinned about being called a liar. Closer partnerships have been built on ground less steady. Anyway, Ames was six feet under by the time I came to that conclusion, so I couldn't ask him if I was right.

We didn't waste time and horse fodder asking around about Bob Squire. Those that knew him by sight liked him, by and large, and weren't eager to help out the enemy. We told them a stretcher instead: We were looking for a red-headed woman who'd run off from her husband, a stock trader well set-up in his profession, over a misunderstanding, and he'd offered a reward of a hundred dollars for information that would lead to her return. So if you want to be accurate, you'd have to say that Ike St. John's first manhunt was a hunt for a woman.

We hadn't a strict likeness of Clara, posing for pictures being about as common locally as pearl-diving, so we showed around a cigarette card with a picture of Helena Modjeska performing in "East Lynne." There wasn't that much of a resemblance, but the yards of silk and lace she posed in would appeal to the female companion of a desperado with his share of twenty thousand to spend. It wouldn't occur to Clara to be invisible just because they were on the run, and Bob wouldn't be Bob if he didn't go along. Anyway the women we showed it to spent more time studying the dress than the face, and the men to any woman who didn't look like she just got back from slopping hogs.

We got a nibble in Sallisaw, though we didn't hardly credit it on account of it was less than thirty miles from Fort Smith, which was bold even for Bob, but we followed it through, and sure enough a couple of skinny boys catfishing the crick there told us a lady dressed like the woman in the picture passed them that morning in a buckboard loaded with portmanteaux, headed north on the crick road. Ames gave them each a penny for the information and to keep their mouths shut and we took off that way, leading our horses and not conversing; that Brushy Mountain country grows boulders like Tennessee grows tobacco, and we weren't counting on Bob being so much in love with peace he wouldn't plant himself behind one to wing us when we showed. That was the *best* case; I never killed a man before that business in Miami, nor would I have bet I ever would, so there was no predicting how our man would react to close pursuit, with a woman to look out for besides. So that slowed us down, and we missed them in Stilwell; but we found their buckboard. The livery operator there said a man and woman answering their descriptions traded him even up for a celerity wagon he'd bought at auction, mostly for collecting firewood as the thoroughbraces were shot and it was stripped down practically to the bed. He'd given them a pair of mules and ten dollars for their played-out team.

That was good news and bad: We knew now we were on the right trail, but the hasty transaction meant they'd either tumbled to the fact they were being followed or sensed it, and when a rabbit dives into the briars it makes double the work for the fox. The livery man didn't know which way they went from there, and the two hotels in town hadn't registered anyone in a week. However, the woman who clerked the general merchandise looked at the picture and said it wasn't her, but she'd sold a sack of Arbuckle's and a brush-and-comb set to a lady dressed as high-toned, who asked if she knew of a place in town where she could get a heel put back on a pump; she said no, but there was a good bootmaker in Tahlequah. From the lady's reaction, the clerk guessed that's where she was headed. No sign of a male companion, but then there wouldn't be if Bob was spooked.

Ames and me palavered. Tahlequah was where the Cherokee legislature sat, and where federal men were met with respect, but rarely cooperation when it came to an investigation in their back yard. We were discussing whether the safest course would be to wire Fort Smith from there for help, in case the rough element decided it was open season on marshals. Bob and Clara were moving at a clip, so we didn't figure we needed to pay close attention to the road ahead while we hashed it out. That was a mistake.

We'd just decided to put off deciding till we got to town

when a sycamore twig snapped half a yard from my left ear and then I heard the report. Bob had taken the lead away from us.

We bailed out of the saddle and took to the scrub, yanking our long guns out of their scabbards and leaving the horses to wander. In the process two more slugs kicked up gravel at our heels; that was just Bob showing off his marksmanship. If he thought it couldn't be avoided, he'd have drilled us through the heart at whatever distance.

Things got quiet then, and we let the birds return to their singing while we looked for where the shots had come from. When my hat tore off my head I thought, *That's Bob*; but it was Ames snatched it off one-handed and skimmed it into the road. The next slug made it jump, and a patch of black-powder smoke slid out from a stand of sassafras at the top of the hill next to the road. Ames shouldered his Spencer and me my Henry and we put two that way. Quiet after that: It was certain Bob wasn't there any more unless he was hit, which I thought unlikely; he'd've moved to another position before my hat hit the ground.

"What was wrong with yours?" I whispered, harsh. I'd just bought that hat in Fort Smith.

"Stampede string." Ames fingered the strap under his chin that kept the old black slouch-brim on his head.

I wouldn't want to repeat that afternoon, though of course I did plenty of times: Keeping the peace is one part shooting and hoorawing and nine parts sitting still while the skeeters bite and sweat burns your eyes and your muscles cramp and the back of your neck prickles on account of your target may have worked his way around behind you, but if you turn to look he might see the movement and open a third eye in your forehead; all for two dollars per arrest and six cents a mile traveling expenses. But I guess it wasn't any social diversion for Bob neither.

And where was Clara? That back-shooting maneuver might be beneath Bob, but women don't wobble between fair and foul when it comes to surviving: They're unreasonable that way. You can see it don't pay to think too much in that situation, and why you need to avoid getting into it in the first place. If you can.

As it turned out, though, we sweated off five pounds each for no good reason except it gave Clara Hornbeck two hours to make it the rest of the way to Tahlequah with the celerity and the swag. Bob kept us pinned down that long, and then he sang out, tossed that long-range Remington rifle and a .36 Navy Colt into the road, and we held our fire while he stepped out of the trees with his hands high. That's when I first laid eyes on Robert Anthony Wayne Squire, all ears and no chin in old overalls and a greasy wool cap so Clara could wear ruffles and stays.

She was good for it, though, because after Judge Parker sent him to the Detroit House of Corrections, a band in burlap hoods blew up the tracks outside Springfield, Missouri, and took him off the train while the escorting marshals were still gathering their wits about them. A porter who saw the bandit holding Bob's mount for him said he was undersize and hitched his hips when he walked. You can make what you want of that, but since no one ever swore to have caught sight of either Bob or Clara in the Nations later, Ames and I agreed them rounds he spent on the road to Tahlequah were a sound investment; though I never did forgive him for my hat.

1926

Buck Jones, Rawlings thought, would approve of the saga of Clara and Bob. It offered all the action, romance, and heroic sacrifice of *Romeo and Juliet,* without the tragedy that sent cinemagoers home in a black study. But the cowboy star would insist on casting himself as Squire, opposite some sylph with bobbed hair and bee-stung lips as the Hornbeck woman; and where would that leave St. John? As little as Rawlings knew of movie manufacture, he knew more about men like Kennedy; having accepted the premise of *Iron Star,* the captain of industry would surely insist on the original pig, minus the poke.

Nothing in his notes suggested how much credit Rawlings had placed in St. John's story at the time. Now it read like something from *The Boy's Book of Buffalo Bill,* complete with a breathless heroine and a Robin Hood in the rough. The marshal had been "playing to the rubes": spinning the kind of yarn the eastern newspapers gobbled up like tinned peaches.

Chloe Ziegler, of whom Rawlings heard much from his companions, had slept with outlaws and lawmen and sold them both out, each to the other; the house she ran in the badlands north of Santa Fe wouldn't have stood a month if she'd behaved as the tender-hearted harlot of St. John's tale. She was old at forty, and if she'd tried to swaddle herself in satin and velvet it would only draw attention to her bad teeth and the bags under her eyes; but as Wild Bill Edwards said, "There was more to Chloe than just powder and paint. Anyway, they all of 'em look like Lillie Langtry in the dark."

To make ends meet, the New Mexico madam sold liquor on the Jicarilla Apache reservation—a federal offense—and did some sharp horse-trading when bandits came through looking for mounts. (Everyone agreed she did better business in that one spot than they did kicking up dust in three territories.) But she sank one well too many. A year after the Buckner affair, based on information supplied by Pinkerton's, the pinewood bungalow was singled out as a way station in the white slave trade. Although no evidence was found, the residents were forced to vacate and a padlock was placed on the door. The proprietress of the house packed up her traps and faded into the desert.

No one ever knew what became of these creatures. None of the census records of the time took note of who they were or where they went. For every Clara Hornbeck who drifted away with her fabled prince, a hundred Chloe Zieglers lay dead and buried without a stone to mark their passage.

St. John had provided this last part of his narrative in pieces, repeating himself frequently and paying little heed to the order of events. The posse had left the train at Elephant Crossing— once a metropolis, on the evidence of exposed foundations and free-standing chimneys, now a prairie-dog town with a human population in single digits—spoken with the railroaders who'd witnessed the robbery, and drawn their horses from the stock car. Hours of sedentary travel had seized up their joints and slowed the function of their arteries: They mounted stiffly and rode on pins and needles the first quarter-mile. Circulation restored, they assumed the roles assigned to them, automatically and without discussion: George American Horse reading the trail, St. John calling upon his vaunted second sight, Edwards charming the locals in the towns and hamlets they passed through, and Pierce on the prowl for ripe young women whose souls required rescue; his value to the enterprise would reveal itself only when blood was shed. Rawlings kept the chronicle. His notes, scribbled using his pommel for a desk, were scattered and smudged, with addenda crabbed into the margins alongside reminders to freshen supplies and provisions. He'd been elected quartermaster, without regard to his opinion on the matter. Clearly he was disenfranchised pending evidence of his own place in the arrangement, a position he shared with the Mexicans.

It wasn't company he'd have chosen. To say that the pair reeked was inadequate. Unwashed flesh and the beans they ate last week seemed hardly to answer for so unholy a stench; and the way they rode, slouched in their saddles far behind the others, one hand on the reins, suggested conspiracy. They would ride for hours in silence, then plunge into a brief, brittle exchange in their bastard dialect. The Pinkerton, taking this as a signal for action, would brace himself, and when it didn't come was disappointed. They might merely have been passing judgment on the scenery; which in any case was nothing to inspire poetry. It was a monotonous journey through flat, arid scrubland, unbroken except by the marshal's reminiscences.

5

THE BATTLE OF THE BOG

I was drawing my pay—sweetened up a little by the sale of confiscated whiskey—half a year before I came to see the inside of Parker's court. I'd helped escort a Chickasaw mixblood called Sam Crosstree over the line from Texas, where he operated a rum shop open and legal; by which I mean the white side of him was too yellow to test the law against serving liquor in the Nations, but on the red side he was shrewd enough to hang out his shingle next door. The Judge would've ignored him as small coin except for the unevenness of the count between those patrons that drank there and left and them that never made it out. Some of us blamed the poison he sold for the general display of bad temper that took place under his roof; but the plain truth is Sam was too lazy or lily-livered to settle an argument before it turned to slaughter.

Well, that was no business of ours unless something happened to make the trip worth getting a warrant, which was required in order to take him back across the border.

He came through for us in December '76.

Jenny Umber shared his bed, scrubbed the floors, and fried corn fritters for the clientele, and wouldn't kill a rat if she caught it eating the last potato in the bin. She was charitable, too: When Sam wasn't looking, she'd feed down-at-luck drifters out the back door. I can't say as that was what set him off, but this one night *some*thing did, and he snatched up a kitchen knife and used it to cut her head almost clean off her shoulders.

I was in Idabel at the time, just across the Red River, on a cold trail with a Choctaw officer named Joe Sky, and it didn't take us ten minutes after we caught wind of the atrocity to decide that making a three-hundred-mile round trip to Fort Smith just for a piece of paper was a waste of horseflesh when we were close enough to spit in Sam's eye. In case Parker balked, there was always the chance our man would attempt a break, and we had a remedy for that. I was willing to let him try, though I can't answer for where Joe Sky stood on the issue; Indians don't need their own tongue to make them a mystery.

We could have left Sam to the Rangers; but, damn it, he and Jenny were *ours*! You can see how quickly I'd taken to the territory.

Sam's shop was a log affair, twice as long as it was wide and dug another ten or twelve feet into a hill, for storing roots and curing the beer he brewed from chicory and molasses with skunkweed to give it a kick, put up in crocks and bottled in Dr. Sloan's, without always bothering to scrub out the liniment. I figure that accounted for as many dead men as gunplay ever did in his place, but since that took longer, no one could say for sure.

He kept pigs in a barbwire pen west of the cabin, so he wouldn't have had to raise a blister digging a hole for the girl; anyway there was no sign of a grave. I don't know which was worse, the murder or what he done to her after, but neither one did him any credit in our eyes.

A stand of honey locust gave us a good view of the place

from cover. A crooked stovepipe with a tin duncecap on top poked up through the roof, to let out smoke from the still. You could inebriate yourself for free just by standing downwind.

I liked that stovepipe. I wanted to borrow a bucket of coal oil from a neighbor and scramble up on the roof from that hill in back and give Sam a sample of what was waiting for him on the other side, but Joe Sky demurred: The roof was sheet iron, he pointed out; we'd be heard coming sure as spring hail, and a charge of buckshot from below would spoil us both for the Easter dance.

I said I didn't like the idea of rushing the place. There were three horses hitched to the rail, and so at least that many guns inside. "That Cherokee champagne Sam stocks turns yellow dogs into brave men and loyal."

"It also makes 'em piss." The Choctaw tipped his head toward a green-pine privy just a quick sprint from the door; leave it to Sam Crosstree not to exert himself more than ten paces when nature came to call.

I grinned at the suggestion. Of course, a man with all of Texas at his feet can make water anywhere he likes, but even a craven woman-butcher prefers to move his bowels in private. All we had to do was fix up a blind and wait, just like stalking deer. That's how what we done for our wages had come to be called a manhunt.

So we wove us a screen from branches and made ourselves as comfortable as you can on ground hard as raw whiskey to begin with, and frozen to boot; and after a little while it began to snow, big shaggy flakes like goose feathers that stuck to our eyelashes and took their time melting on the barrels of our scabbard guns. We blew our noses on our sleeves, shifted positions from time to time on account of the cramps, and wished we were anyplace else. That's the rip-roaring life you read about in *Ned Buntline's Own*.

A couple of times the shop door opened and we raised our sights, but it was just strangers stepping out to sprinkle the grass; customers, probably wanted somewhere, though not by us. Anyway it broke up the time, which had begun to be considerable.

"I bet he's got a bucket back there behind the bar," I said. "How lazy can you get?"

Joe Sky grunted. "Ossified innards, maybe; a cancer of the stomach. Some fellows have all the luck."

We were losing the light. I was about to suggest we pack it in till morning when light tipped out from inside the shop and Sam came out.

Anyone who knew him only by reputation might expect a brute of a man, all gristle with the hair side turned out; but he could pass for a bookkeeper or a bank teller, slight as to build, bald as a china egg and chin scraped clean: green sleeve garters, by God, and yellow gaiters on his boots. He was trotting towards the privy like a man on a mission; he was quicker than he looked, as I found out soon enough. I drew a bead, but Joe Sky put a hand on the receiver. "Catch him when he comes out," he said. "Be like picking a bottle off a fencerail."

"If it ain't too dark by then." But I lowered the Henry.

Well, the sun slid down and it was twilight, and it started to look like we'd have to wait till he came back out and passed in front of the lit window on our side, and there were too many things could go wrong with that plan.

I got up on my elbows. "Cover me, I'm going in."

Joe Sky assumed the position, elbows on the ground and

his buttstock snug to his shoulder. He wasn't one to waste words on an argument.

I stepped out of the woods, cutting a half-moon to take advantage of the shade, as one of Sam's patrons might have took up a post at the window with a weapon in his fist. That was good until the last ten feet, where a strip of starlight made me a clear target, which was where I had to rely on the Choctaw's judgment. He didn't have to be a crack shot, just pepper the side of the building to make a distraction; but I hadn't spent enough time in his company to know anything about his sense of timing. Anyway he didn't shoot, and neither did anybody else, right up to when I yanked open the outhouse door and pumped a slug blind into the middle of the blackness inside. There wasn't room in it for a fruit bat to duck.

I stepped aside then, in case Sam wasn't dead enough to hold his fire, and I couldn't count on Joe Sky to back me up because my shot would've woken them up inside the shop, and there I'd be caught in crossfire. I levered in another round, spun on my heel, and threw down on the occupying party, but just enough light seeped in through the cracks to show there wasn't any, and nothing but an empty hole where he was supposed to sit. All I'd managed to do with my shot was knock a board out of the back wall.

I lowered the Henry; which nearly cost me my skin, because just then Sam Crosstree popped up through that hole and dropped the hammer on a ball-and-percussion Remington all the way around the cylinder at point-blank range.

I had to assign him points for being clever enough to reckon he was being laid in wait for, and to crawl down into the pit and wait for whoever it was to lose patience and force the issue; but also to take some off for exposing his powder to all that piss and shit so it wouldn't ignite. Six shots, six misfires, and there I stood like a split finger. If the good Lord in His mercy gave me as many lives as a cat, that leaves me just the one.

So there Sam was, covered with muck, holding that useless gun, eyes big and white as cueballs, and dead where he stood. But as little respect as I had for the man, I was impressed by his invention, and tickled pink to still be alive, so instead of plugging him I swung my buttstock at his head. He dropped like—well, like a turd—and if it hadn't been for his elbows stopping him on the edge of that hole I'd have had to stoop down and drag him up out of it by his ears. As it was, he was trouble enough by the time I got him outside, still limp, and me near as filthy from the contact.

Joe Sky, having settled his mind on the subject of my continued good health, had attended to business: He had three men from inside the shop sitting on the ground, trussed up like capons. He looked down at Sam, pinching his nose.

"Jesus Christ, Ike!" he said. "It wasn't enough just to arrest him, you had to take a dump on him too?"

6

THE BENCH AND THE BROADAXE

You had to duck under its beams to get around, but a lot of people done it, in the half-story attic of the old courthouse in Fort Smith. They came just to look at an ordinary kitchen knife with a plain wood handle and six inches of steel blade wore down paper-thin, from chopping the heads off catfish and cutting up turnips for the hogs. For a long time it was the main attraction in Judge Parker's cabinet of curiosities. I was the one put it there.

It was never entered in evidence, as I couldn't swear it was the same knife Sam Crosstree used to decapitate poor Jenny Umber; but it was the only thing in his kitchen that looked as if it would serve the purpose, so I wrapped it in a piece of oilcloth and toted it all the way from Texas, along with Sam in bruises and bracelets. It shared the space with other oddities, including a pair of fine yellow boots for the possession of which Daniel Evans blew the brains out of a boy named Seabolt, the axe Lewis Burrows used to split up his father-in-law over an unpaid debt of thirty-five cents, and the stolen watch that hanged Dick Spanish for the cowardly murder of Deputy U.S. Marshal Royal Ames during the performance of his duty in Pheasant's Bluff.

The Judge said he got the idea for the exhibit from an inspector visiting from Scotland Yard, who told him about the Black Museum back in London. He intended it for the enlightenment of would-be lawbreakers, as each item represented a man who'd died on the gallows. I can't say what become of the collection after the new courthouse was built; thrown out, likely, or broken up by personnel and taken home for souvenirs; we don't worship such things here as they do in the old country. But I'm proud of my contribution.

When I learned I was to testify at Sam's trial, I bought a cutaway coat and striped trousers from a clothier on Garrison Avenue who specialized in fitting out deputies for court; he redeemed the merchandise afterward at a discount and sold it back to them next time at full price. (The court was Fort Smith's main industry: Ask that haberdasher; also the carpenters who built the coffins for the condemned and the hotel and boarding house operators who rented rooms to pilgrims crowded into town for the show.) I broke in the suit of clothes along with a haircut and took a seat in the back row of the gallery to see how things shook down when court was in session.

The room took up the northeast half of the ground floor in the old army barracks, and resembled the inside of a cigar box, with red-cedar panels that gave off a cozy smell when the windows were shut in winter, rows of bentwood chairs for the spectators, and a long table shared by the principals on both sides of the trial. In those days there was nothing to separate the Judge's big cherrywood desk from the rest of the room, but after a farmer accused of killing his neighbor in a duel made an attack on the man behind it, an oak rail was installed to slow down any further attempts. From morning till dark, six days a week for twenty-one years, Parker sat there in his leather-bottomed chair, hearing evidence and swinging his gavel at every least ripple of unrest in the gallery.

I don't know what I was expecting: Maybe one of his famous come-to-Jesus charges to the jury, full of God and Providence and man's responsibility to his brother, leading up to a guilty verdict and then one of those fire-and-brimstone orations that earned him the name Old Thunder: ". . . there to be hanged by the neck until you are dead, dead, *dead*!" It always got the same reaction, no matter how many times you heard it: Silence as loud as a boiler blowing its top, then a whoosh of breath let out from fifty throats at once. After that the gavel seemed unnecessary.

But that day I was disappointed. From the time I sat down till the time I got up and left, the attorneys were locked in hoarse conference with the Judge over some fine print in the statutes while the audience cleared its throat and squirmed on its fanny and the little gray man in the witness chair at the end of the desk looked as miserable as a dog hitched out in the rain. I gathered he was the defendant; but whether he was accused of cutting a tinker's throat or of stealing a pine knot from a woodbox, I didn't stick around long enough to find out. If this was how things went when Sam Crosstree was on the spit, I thought, I'd as soon watch a Chinaman wash a shirt.

Well, it wasn't, as I learned two weeks later. Some of the other marshals had done their homework, rounding up witnesses who'd heard Sam roaring threats at poor Jenny Umber half a mile off, and one who saw him burying a pair of bloodstained overalls in his yard, and when Fred Ostler, as good a man behind the badge as he was at a fish fry, held up that same garment in front of the jury and told where he'd dug it up, the sensation it made went through the roof and near broke the Judge's wrist pounding it down. After that, what Joe Sky and I had to say about the shithouse fight came off tame; though I was a season living down the laughter. Even Parker, strait-laced as he was, covered his mouth to defend his dignity.

The mood lasted only until a midwife neighbor of Sam and Jenny's took the stand. The stories she told about that sweet girl, her Christian charity, and the purity of her voice when she sang in church, brought out the hankies like pennants on the Fourth of July. The defense lawyer tried to shake her, but she stuck her ground. Two chairs down from me I saw a Fort Smith farrier famous for pitching an anvil clear across First Street on a dare wipe his eyes with a sleeve.

Meanwhile Sam sat behind that long table with a face struck from stone. All the time Ostler was telling about the human bones he found in the pig pen—including the gold tooth that rested the prosecution's case—that rum-peddling son of a bitch sat picking at his fingernails in his lap, bored as a fly on a window ledge. He yawned once; raise my right hand.

The jury was out twenty minutes, half as long as the Judge spent instructing them; I reckon they played a rubber or two of euchre there in the back room for decency's sake. The foreman, a skinny store clerk with muttonchops out to here and one of those Adam's apples you can't help but watch bob up and down when they talk, drove the first nail in Sam's coffin, and Parker done the rest, in that ringing voice you never forgot—weeping at the end, I swear; bitterer tears no one ever shed. Sam's face didn't move a muscle.

I stayed home the day of the hanging. You know my position on that. He went through the trap unaccompanied, and I hear the doctor whose job it was to check his signs had to wait half an hour for the heart to stop beating before he signed the death certificate. If so it was one of the few times Maledon was less than efficient. He couldn't have picked a better case for carelessness.

I promised to tell you about Maledon. He was a scrawny little German with a white beard near half his size, who killed his first felon long before he handled his first rope. He was a Crawford County deputy sheriff and a deputy U.S. Marshal both, in which capacity he shot an escaping prisoner to death with a single round at a distance of sixty yards. That was the first of five. Impressed, Parker offered him the job no one wanted, and he done it for a hundred dollars a pop until the court was dissolved in '96, outlasting six Presidents. And he attended all the capital trials—studying the customer, I guess, calculating his weight and the strength or weakness of his neck. He was a scientist, and the prince of hangmen. A hundred years ago he'd have been one of those officers of the court that took pride in separating a man from his head with one blow of the axe.

I saw him sitting in on Sam Crosstree's proceedings, back in the corner Bailiff Winston reserved just for him. I didn't know who he was then, but you couldn't look at him when he was at his forge—them slow-burning eyes of his fixed on the front of the room—combing his whiskers with his fingers, and not take notice. They were long, those fingers; tapered like a pianist's but spreading at the tips, like a frog's, so that whatever they touched they stuck to tight, come wind or flash flood. They say he used only the best Kentucky hemp, and spent hours oiling it with linseed till it was supple enough to whirl around a man's neck and come up slap against the spine, *crack*! Like a cherry bomb going off.

Brrr! I get the whim-whams just talking about it, knowing it was only by a shift in Parker's mood—one moment in his fourteen-hour day when a notion ticked his ear, playful-like—that I wasn't one of Little George's customers. But I don't regret my part in introducing Sam Crosstree to him—even though poor Jenny might disapprove, sweet forgiving girl that she was.

1926

A fold of faded pink paper spilled out of the next notebook Rawlings opened; it fell into four pieces when he opened it. It was an advertisement, printed in letterpress and bordered with crudely drawn silhouettes of sixguns:

WARDLE'S METROPOLITAN COSMOGRAPH
MARVEL OF THE CENTURY

SEE!

Desperadoes locked in deadly combat with the law!

SEE!

Galloping horses!

SEE!

Red-hot "six-shooters" spitting smoke and fire!

SEE!

A runaway stagecoach hurtling toward YOU!

SEE!

It all as if you were there

All in the comfort and safety of your seat!

All-motion!

All-action!

All authentic!

★ ★ ★

BONUS PRESENTATION:

George M. Cohan's

New Revue
Direct from Broadway!
All for the Price of
5¢
!!!!!!

The Princess Playhouse

114 7th Street
Kansas City, Kansas

Shows continuous from 10:00 A.M. to 7:00 P.M.
Every Day Except Sunday

The ink was blurred, and some of the letters nearly obliterated where his thumbs had gouged the damp paper. It still smelled of mildew, although it had had twenty years to dry.

He'd forgotten that day entirely; he thought it ironic that he should be reminded of it now that he was part of what Buck Jones referred to pompously as "the motion-picture industry." From what he'd seen of its more recent output, he couldn't see that the technology had developed very far. The printing press and the washing machine had left it well behind.

The Colorado north country had greeted the posse with driving rain: "Piss out of a boot," was St. John's assessment, and even Rawlings, who'd been brought up to assign profanity to the lower classes, thought it an appropriate characterization. Icy, gluey, and relentless, it streamed off their hatbrims and crept around the edges of their slickers, soaking them to the bone. When they dismounted to lead their exhausted horses, they slipped and sank to their ankles in slimy clay, feet squishing in their boots with a noise like a pump sucking oil. "Where's Noah now we need him?" Bill Edwards asked of no one in particular.

The deluge kept up for three days, in the middle of which they straggled into a camp belonging to a team of hired prospectors, where an accommodating straw boss invited them into the workers' mess—he called it the "commissary"—to thaw their insides with oyster stew and gallons of coffee piping hot. He shook his head at all of St. John's questions: He and his crew had been working day and night collecting ore samples to be sent to Denver—they'd given up on silver and were testing for zinc—and couldn't be expected to pay much attention to strangers drifting by, be they outlaws or peddlers or preachers riding the circuit; but the lawmen were free to interview his crew, if they didn't take too much time from digging.

The shelter was the most substantial in the tent village, built of corrugated iron, the air inside gummy with the stench of wet flannel, rubber galoshes, cigar exhaust, expectorated tobacco, and every possible vintage of perspiration. As his eyes grew accustomed to the lantern light, Rawlings saw rows of rough pine benches and trestle tables and a great iron cookstove keeping the kettles hot and drawing steam from union suits strung on a line, contributing their share to the close atmosphere.

Just inside the entrance stood a metal table supporting a foreign assembly of gears and pulleys. A man stood there sorting through some clanking items in a stiff leather case braced on one raised knee. He wore an argyle pullover and a tweed cap with the bill twisted over one ear; as out of place a figure in that company of men in muddy overalls as Rawlings felt in his.

Seeing the direction of his guests' gaze, the straw boss shouted over the rain roaring on the roof. "That's the Cosmograph!"

"It sure is!" St. John might merely have been pretending not to have heard him.

The straw boss shook his head and tapped the edge of the pink sheet the marshal was holding; he'd handed one to each of the visitors.

The marshal looked up from the sheet and bellowed in his ear. "I don't know any more than when I asked! Who the hell's Wardle and what the hell's a Cosmograph?"

"Some kind of inventor. He invented a plow that wouldn't pull and an aeroplane that didn't fly. The Cosmograph's the first thing he made that works. It's a pip."

"Well, I don't feature spending a nickel on it, with or without the grub."

"It's on the company! Nobody said nothing about it being just for the workers. All I'm to do is hand out these here flyers. You couldn't have picked a better day to wander in! Load up your trenchers and we'll get started!"

"What is it, some kind of theater show?"

But the rain had stepped up, making communication impossible. The straw boss nodded as if he agreed with whatever St. John had said, slapped him on the back, and moved on among the benches to distribute flyers.

The stew tasted of lime and rust from the water it was brewed in, also of whatever had happened to fall into the kettle from above, where barn swallows fluttered, but it was hearty and hot; the steam from Edwards' bowl fogged the lenses of his spectacles. Rawlings scalded his tongue on the coffee. Pierce mouthed some kind of grace and swamped out his bowl with a thick slab of cornbread, polishing it to a high shine; quite apart from his other habits, all of his appetites were disturbingly prodigious. George American Horse provisioned himself at the serving-table and retired to a deserted section of the mess—from long habit, Rawlings supposed; for some white westerners, the Little Big Horn was just last week, and even a brave must choose his battles. But then the Pinkerton's own jury was still out on the bunch of them, the Indian included.

Spoons were scraping crockery when a laborer took his place on a folding stool at the front of the room; there a bed-sheet hung from a truss overhead. He unlatched a concertina and sat waiting while the man in the gaudy sweater swung open a panel in the back of the Cosmograph, struck a match, and inserted it through the aperture. Acetylene ignited with a *plop* and a bright shaft shot the length of the room and splashed across the bedsheet. He fixed a crank to the side of the machine and began turning; it made a ratcheting sound like a windlass and the squeezebox commenced to play.

The worker sat kitty-corner to the bedsheet with one eye cocked that direction, timing his performance to the shadow play taking place there; when revolvers belched smoke, he squeezed a series of shrill notes, simulating reports, and ma-nipulated the bellows furiously, elbows pumping, during a horse race through a canyon. It was all very realistic—except for the canyon, which clearly was painted canvas—and the audience hooted and stamped its feet for ten delirious min-utes as bandits looted a Butterfield coach of its express box, robbed the passengers, shot the shotgun messenger, started the team galloping, and leapt into their saddles with a posse in hot pursuit; the gun battle at the climax nearly upset both the musician and the stool supporting him. When the pilot-less coach came thundering straight into the shaft of light, the men seated on the front bench shouted and rolled out of harm's way. Both Menéndezes scrambled for the Winchesters in their laps; they were never without them. Edwards, who sat beside the pair, threw a long arm across both their chests, stopping them before the carbines cleared the table and possibly saving a life or two.

The argyle man stopped cranking. The screen became a bedsheet once again.

The straw boss appeared at the end of their bench. He was a corpulent man who wore his badge of office, a red necktie, tucked into the waistband of his trousers. "What'd you fellows think?" The rain had subsided to a steady drumming, allowing the conversation to resume at a normal level.

Pierce broke his customary silence. "Witchcraft! It blasphemes the Lord's will!"

"Exciting, though," Edwards said. "I think George messed his pants."

"*Hough!*" It was the closest the Indian ever came to sounding like a stage savage.

One of the Mexicans muttered something to his companion; but it was St. John who responded.

"*Quién sabe, amigo. Magia del este.* Magic from back East. Mr. Pinkerton?" Reflection from the screen washed the left side of the marshal's face in light. The effect was satanic.

"Something I saw once in school. It wouldn't interest you."

"Don't tease. It's not in your character."

"Very well. You're in charge." Rawlings cleared his throat; he felt a cold coming on. "I watched a boy drop a mouse down a girl's blouse in third grade. I used to imagine what it would have been like with ten mice and ten girls. Now I know."

George, as it turned out, spent the night more comfortably than his companions, in his bedroll on the duckboard floor behind the cookstove, warm and dry and sequestered, to preserve the purity of the Caucasian race; the rest split up to share accommodations with the workers in their tents, all of which leaked and most of whose residents took turns snoring and passing wind. And it was George, the next day, who found one who remembered seeing the Buckner gang pass the camp a week past; he was a Negro, paired with another in a tent pitched by the latrine, and not one to serve judgment on a stranger based on the shade of his skin. Too, he was a veteran of the Tenth Cavalry—colored soldiers in the campaigns against the plains tribes—and able to communicate with the Crow in sign language; a distinct benefit to a posse concerned with discretion: The combined reward offered for the bandits' capture—alive if possible, but anyway for sure—came to ten thousand dollars, and the competition was fierce enough as it was.

"How is it he knows it's them he saw?" St. John asked George. The party had met to compare notes on the edge of a dry wash where their mounts were picketed; it was dry no longer, and running swift as a river. The rain had stopped at last, but there would be hazards on the road ahead, mudslides and washouts, and lakes where there should be open prairie.

"Jim Shirley. You notice a man with stumps instead of hands. He had that Indian woman with him too, the one looks after his guns, buttons his fly and like that. My man was on a break, taking a leak, when they came by leading their horses. Him being colored, I guess they thought he couldn't understand plain English. It's an advantage him and I have you don't," he added, poker-faced.

"Never mind that. Say where they were headed?"

"One of them said something about Carol expecting them in Pinto Creek by the twentieth."

"Where's that?" Rawlings said.

St. John looked at him. "Half-day's ride from Laramie."

Rawlings seethed. Of course a Pinkerton based in Chey-enne would know that. Why had the Agency added that straw to his back?

"Twentieth of what month?" St. John said to George. "That's three hundred miles."

"Closer four. I'm just telling you what he said."

Rawlings felt the need to contribute something. "He's just trying to throw us off track."

"If he is, it isn't for the reward, or he wouldn't still be here busting rocks."

"Who's Carol, you think?" said St. John. "I never knew a sporting woman worth riding more than half a day just for a tumble."

"My man didn't ask."

"What's the trail say?" Edwards said.

"After that rain?"

The marshal directed his gaze north. Rawlings wondered if he was consulting his famous crystal ball. Then he turned his face to the sun.

"Rawlings is right, though not about the colored. Race and his boys are safe as houses up in that Hole-in-the Wall country: He knows it and so do I. I'm supposed to think he wouldn't be that obvious, and go on west looking to pick up his scent while he turns north. It's a question of which fist the penny's in this time. Up to a point it's a compliment."

The Pinkerton shook his head. "No one is as famous as you think you are. How do you know he knows it's you on his trail, or for that matter if anyone is?"

"I won't explain. You wouldn't credit it if I did."

George turned his face into the wind. "I smell snow. We'll need gear."

"We can get it in Denver."

"Wasn't that where we was headed before we left the train?" said Edwards.

7

SWAMI IKE

You're right to ask if I'm as famous as I think, since there's nothing easier to forget than a busted politician; but for a while there I couldn't pass a saloon anywhere in the territory without starting a riot, everybody wanting to be first to buy me a drink. I doubt Jennings Bryan could attract a bigger crowd than me just after Sam Crosstree paid his debt to the devil.

Like I said, Judge Parker was cinched in mighty tight, and all that buzz about Sam making his stand in a privy stung him because of the disrespect he thought it brung to the court just when he was fighting to overcome its reputation as a lynching station; so he put me on a month's paid leave and indicated he wouldn't object if I took advantage of the time to travel. Fort Smith just then was top-heavy with scribblers from the eastern press sniffing after fresh copy, so I guessed he wouldn't mind if I made myself rare game. That backfired in the end, but we couldn't know that. Anyway he was boss, so I loaded a packhorse with bacon and dried apples and set to wandering.

Where to go was no puzzle. I'd never been upcountry beyond the North Fork, and the way things were going the whole United States of America would be settled by sodbusters and gasfitters before I could see it if I didn't go now, so I struck the Northern Trail to Dakota Territory.

Deadwood was lively: Custer was fresh dead, the Sioux and Cheyenne were riding the high country to Canada with the whole army on their tail, and all the talk around the poker tables was of that and Wild Bill Hickok, shot in the back five months before I arrived by a yellow dog named McCall, and him sprung by a miners' court; well, that made the place noisier than ever, what with some hardrock miner striking a new lode of silver every Sunday and standing perfect strangers to drinks till you fell off the footrail. It got stale fast; also there in the Black Hills in January the sun goes down at lunchtime, and all the lilac water in all the whorehouses won't cure a case of melancholy in a man when it's dark that early. So I scraped what I'd managed to keep from the cardsharps into my hat and took off into the snow country where a man can breathe; provided you don't sear your lungs taking it in.

That part of the territory is celebrated for its grass, growing head-high for thousands of acres and green as the first frog of spring; only you couldn't prove it by me, because when I came to it both horses were up to their withers in snow, with the wind blowing it into clouds and the sun slamming down on all that white so fierce I spent my first week in Bismarck blind as a mole, holed up in a hotel with a tea-leaf poultice on my lids to draw the pain; that on the advice of a doctor whose specialty was miseries of the eye—and he wasn't starving that season.

When the bandanna came off and I saw what kind of shelter I'd stumbled into, I checked out and moved into a place where the roaches didn't winter and the roof didn't leak. Still, it wasn't the Palmer House. The city had been on the map less than two years, and the Northern Pacific wasn't likely to bring anything like refinement for another five, despite all the construction: saws wheezing, hammers clattering, and carpenters cussing in German from sunup to sundown, and sometimes late as midnight when the moon fell on the snow. I never liked the sound since Mexico, with my gallows going up right outside the jail.

The town had a watering-hole and a house of God, of course; where the first takes root, the second's sure to sprout. I don't see where all this talk in church about legislating the gin house out of existence is going to gain traction when the one can't get along without the other. But the minute I stepped inside the sampling room of the Acropolis Hotel I knew I'd misjudged the pace of civilization: stained-glass fixtures, salmon and Sauerkraut on beds of crushed ice, a mahogany bar as long as a packet-boat, and a flock of fat naked women playing ring-the-rosy with a goat-man in a frame behind it. It was still morning, so the clamshell piano on the stage wasn't in use, but it was painted gold and white, so it was still entertaining.

Whatever happened to places like the Acropolis, I wonder? I was in Bismarck again last year, scouting for campaign contributions, and was lucky to draw a beer with no more head on it than the idiot son of a senator, with a newspaper picture of Anna Held tacked to the wall for decoration. The hotel had been torn down to make room for a coal yard. Everything went to hell after we took Cuba.

I commend that hour for visiting a saloon of the Acropolis type. There weren't more than a half-dozen customers sprinkled throughout, three drinking at tables normally reserved for cards, one at the opposite end of the bar and the rest grazing at the sideboard. The faro man was playing Patience. The bartender, in a striped shirt and butterfly tie, came over on the trot. "What'll it be?" And I knew right then all that build-up was more than just show. A fancy bottle can as soon hold spirits of ammonia as French champagne, but this gent took pride in the fare.

We went into conference, at the end of which I sprang for the Sean O'Farrell, which was a mick name for a shot of rye with a beer chaser, intended for the sons of Erin that built the railroad, but after one sip of the whiskey I told him to bring another round to a table by the window and leave the bottle. It was genuine Kentucky, with no bark on it. He even let me open a tab, me with my unfamiliar face.

In a little while a boy came in peddling *The Dakotan*, a local sheet, and I was reading about the wrassling match over the presidential election when I got interrupted.

"Mister St. John?"

Which is no small thing to hear when you're new in town and have enemies on both sides of the badge. Them days I carried my Army .44 on my left hip for the cross-draw, after Hickok, and I had it cocked and under the stranger's chin before my chair finished tipping over.

"We ain't just been properly introduced." I was proud of my choice of words; I hadn't even had time to prepare anything.

The man smiled. He was constructed like a ham, narrow at the top and broad about the middle, with brown wiry whiskers that spilled over his chin, down his neck, and under his collar, which was none too clean; and he wore a greasy bowler hat screwed down tight with his hair springing out under the brim all around. His bearskin coat hung to his shoe tops, open to show the black-and-orange checks of his town suit. He looked like someone had gone to skin a grizzly and found a sewing-machine salesman underneath.

"Beg pardon," he said; and his Adam's apple didn't move

more than a quarter-inch either direction, with that muzzle making a dent in the bottom rung of his double chin. "I came in half-cocked. I have a card."

He had it ready, with his arm bent. I gave him room to swallow and reached across with my left hand to take it. It was printed in raised letters on quality stock and said:

J. MERCER FLEET
Journalist
23 Beaver Rd.
Des Moines, Iowa

I said, "I already got a paper, Mr. Fleet. Who says I'm St. John?"

"I was in the gallery in Fort Smith last month, covering the Sam Crosstree trial for the Chicago *Herald*; I saw you testify. I recognized you coming in here. I'm in town reporting on the progress of the railroad for the *Frontier Index*. I thought I'd try my luck at an exclusive interview. Sir, you're news!"

"I never heard of the rag. *Herald* fire you?"

"They never hired me. I'm freelance. The *Index* is the pet pup of the Northern Pacific, got up to feather the nests of Gould and Vanderbilt; you're wasted on them. I intend to wire your story to *Frank Leslie's Illustrated Newspaper* in New York City."

Well, I knew that one. I'd seen copies even in Durango, on sale in adobe stores that carried deep-fried *cucarachas* and ground dried armadillo dicks to stiffen a man's resolve, and in the Nations, where the five civilized tribes traded them among themselves. Bob Squire left a stack behind when he struck camp in haste on the Sallisaw road. I was impressed enough to ship the Colt and invite Fleet to draw up a chair. I righted mine, refilled my pony glass from the bottle of rye, and slid it over.

"Thank you, no," says he. "Whiskey burns my belly. Will you join me in a peach brandy? My treat."

That one was listed second from the top on the chalkboard behind the bar, just under the Philadelphia cherry cordial— at six bits a shot, if you please; I figured you get to take the glass home. I said much obliged and finished my beer to cleanse my palate, as they say.

So we drank, he bought, I talked, and he spoiled piles of foolscap with his Stylograph pen, a marvel of the century, like Mr. Wardle's Cosmograph; it drew ink from its own well if you shook it hard enough. And the more of that eastern applejack I took in, the steeper the tale I told.

That's how it came to be that Jack LeFever got promoted from deadbeat to desperado. Fleet wanted gunfights and truck, but even between us we couldn't sell a shithouse shoot-out to Leslie's readers. The way the hunt for Bob Squire finished, Bob would come out the hero; the Judge wouldn't sit still for that, and since Bob and Clara were still out there someplace I couldn't very well change the ending and risk one or both of 'em breaking cover to call me a liar. I talked about Mexico—selling guns to freedom fighters being more to Fleet's order than robbing trains in Arizona. He lapped that up, the story of a man cheating Díaz's gallows, then coming back home to send Yankee sinners to Parker's. But like they say, "What've you done lately?" So I spun a yarn about a one-man civilian posse taking after that woman-killing fugitive from Nebraska, Jack LeFever, ending after five hundred grueling miles in a slick-draw contest in Miami, which was how

I come to be invited into the company of the U.S. Marshals. It made a neater fit without the unnecessary particulars.

That's when I said that thing about eating what Jack ate and sleeping where he slept, catching his scent that way: Gypsy fortune-teller stuff. Fleet left out the part about whores, *Leslie's* being a family publication, but it worked just as good without it. I sometimes wonder if I'd have got the same inspiration if I'd stuck to plain whiskey.

Well, it's what sold them in New York. "'SWAMI IKE': THE IRON STAR OF PARKER'S COURT TELLS HIS STORY," laid out in letters big as June beetles, with steel-engraved pictures of the bloody crime, a horseback chase through cactus, and the showdown in the livery stable.

I doubt J. Mercer Fleet swallowed a word, but it gave him a career. He was still at it years later, when I threw my hat into the ring. He wrote my autobiography.

8

THE ICE BOX

New York shipments reached Fort Smith at least two days ahead of Bismarck; I put that much together when a telegram found me at my hotel. I'd about forgotten I'd notified the court of my stopping place by wire.

It was brief: Old Thunder never charged the taxpayers a cent more than what was needed.

REPORT IN PERSON WITHOUT DELAY
I C PARKER

That could only mean my write-up had come to his notice. Anything published anywhere in connection with the court was bound to reach his desk. The current edition of *Frank Leslie's Illustrated Newspaper* wouldn't be seen in my part of Dakota for another day or so, a week late; but there could be no other explanation for my sudden recall. And I didn't think it probable the Judge wanted to shake my hand.

I'd taken in all the scenery I cared to on the ride north, so I sold the packhorse to a livery, bought a ticket at the station, got my chestnut loaded aboard the stock car, and had settled into a chair car with the day's *Dakotan* for company when someone rapped on my window: a well-fed citizen with a red face, a slouch hat, and a star pinned to his overcoat. I pulled down the window, letting in that healthy high plains air to paralyze my nostrils, and said howdy-do.

He asked if I was St. John. He'd a voice to go with his circumference, thick and bubbly like molasses rolling to a boil. I reckoned the mail had come in from the East and now I was famous here too, so there wasn't any point in not admitting it. "Who's asking?"

"Luther Bremen, Burleigh County Deputy Sheriff. Sheriff Yoder's out of town and I need a good man to come with me and make an arrest."

I told him I had business in Fort Smith; but I could see already he wouldn't be argued with. Nothing would do but that the Iron Star come along to see the manacles put on another threat to the public peace. I had a reputation now and it required tending. Notoriety has its annoyances.

"Here in town?" I said, hopeful. I might still make the 12:15 and not have to unload my horse.

He shook his head. "Out Apple Creek way, ten miles or so. Neighbor boy brought the word."

"What's the charge?"

"Murder!"

Some days you can't catch luck with a gunnysack.

"I smell snow," Bremen said, when we were about a mile out.

I wanted to say, well, what's that on the ground? But George said the same thing just yesterday. I never got the nose for it myself, though these days rheumatism serves the same end. But one look at the sky told me there was no point debating the issue: It was gray as Rip's whiskers and laid right on top of last week's snow like a brick.

You've seen that country, even if you've never been: Forty-acre plots set sliced in squares like cornbread in the pan, with barns twice as big as the houses; barns being to German farmers what buffalo was to the Indians. The founders named the town Bismarck to rope them in, Germans having a reputation as solid citizens who paid taxes and didn't go around busting windows on a Saturday night.

Bremen liked to talk. He rode a fine Arabian, long in the croup, with an arch tail. I'd never heard of the animal, which he said he bought at auction; he'd married money, and his wife wanted him to run for sheriff so that when statehood came along she'd be wife of the governor.

By the time we got to the house I had a fair idea of what had taken place there. The boy who'd come to the sheriff's office had been sent by his parents to investigate the ruckus down the road, seen what he'd seen, reported back, and ridden the family mule into town to make things official. He came along with us, a farmboy burnt brown as a boot, with a sedge of yellow hair and no more meat on him than a ham bone in a boarding house. He stayed put while we went inside, weapons in hand.

"Oh, Glory," said the deputy.

He'd interpreted the situation properly based on the boy's account, not that it helped to know it going in: A hefty young woman in a housedress on the kitchen floor, bled out from holes in her throat and chest, and a boy and a girl about nine and ten in similar condition in a bedroom in back. Both rooms still smelled of burnt powder and blood. Bloody shoeprints, wet still, led down a narrow hall to a back door hanging open on its hinges, and tracks in the snow outside to the barn. But before we could start that direction, something commenced to bang. It took us a minute to locate the sound as coming from under our feet.

A narrow door in the kitchen gave onto steep wood steps and a homely smell of potatoes and dirt and salt meat. It was black in the stairwell, so we lit a lamp we found and took it along, leading the way with our pistols, of course; there's nothing to make a man's back crawl like something that don't fit a situation once he thinks he's got it all worked out. Did the husband-father-killer double back on his tracks, or did he leave a partner behind? Either way it looked like somebody was laying in wait for us down there in the dark, with his eyes adjusted to it and ours not.

Bremen hung back on the top step, meaning I should go first. He was breathing shallow. I couldn't charge it against him: Here was he, a deputy sheriff accustomed to locking up drunks and giving kids the boot for sneaking into the grain mill at night to smoke, and here was I, caught bragging about all the untamed parties I brung in to Parker's jail. Strung up by my own suspenders, as you'd say.

That basement was dug only seven feet deep, but the trip down took us a year, and all the time that banging kept up, getting louder with each step. You could breed mushrooms in your throat, the air was that musty, and as cold as it was you heard the sweat sizzling down your neck. The light from our lamp showed bedrock where the shovels had give up, glass jars on timber shelves, a split venison carcass swaying from the beams, a bin heaped with potatoes like great brown blisters, and a big maplewood ice box, which was where the noise was coming from.

An ice box belongs in a kitchen, not a basement; but the door to this one was warped, so it was no good to keep ice in

but still useful for something, storage or splitting up for kindling, so it hadn't got chucked out. The latch was long gone,
replaced with a wood block screwed to the frame so it could
be twisted to hold the door shut. The screw must have been
loose, because it had swung down on its own when whoever
was doing the banging had climbed in and pulled the door
to, trapping him inside.

I grabbed Bremen's arm and steered him that way, telling
him with gestures it was time for him to make himself useful. He set down the lamp and twisted aside the block, using
his off hand, while I stood back ready to shoot. He could
move quick, I'll say that; both our guns were trained on the
ice box when it opened and spilled its contents out onto the
floor.

9

MALEDON LOSES ONE

He said his name was George; Bremen wasn't having any of it, it must be Short Horn or Running Mad, but I told him half the Indians I knew had names just like the rest of us, those tribes in the Nations being civilized. The boy didn't give us any other, and hasn't yet. The American Horse came from me: George, you're welcome.

At the time he fell out of that ice box he was about fourteen, but could pass for ten. The crotch of his overalls hung down to his knees and you could make another pair just from the material turned up at the cuffs. That noodle-gnawing son of a bitch Drebber who killed his own family worked him just for table scraps, and if you know German farm folk they never leave a table but that they roll. George filled out and up later, but if he was a fish the day we met I'd have throwed him back.

He spoke American, probably better than me; still does when he wants to stir me up, but I ran for office, and there's nothing like it for growing a thick hide. His daddy was one of the Crows that scouted for Custer. George got left behind at Fort Lincoln when the Seventh Cavalry pulled out for Montana Territory, and when the news came of the massacre he cut and run, on account of rumors of lynching parties— vengeful whites not bothering to identify friendly Indians from hostiles—and it was more than just rumors. He was forced to go renegade at an age when most boys are just finding out what to do with a hard-on.

Living off the land the way his people showed him, he got as far as Apple Crick when this Drebber caught him sleeping in his barn, but instead of running him through with his potato fork he hired him on as a field hand, which in this case is clodbuster talk for slave. George slept in the loft, and if it wasn't for stealing eggs from the hens he'd have starved to death on just them leftovers that stood for wages. Drebber tried beating him once and got a chunk bit out of his hand for the effort, so the arrangement was temporary at best. George was squirreling away eggs against the day and picking out the fattest pullets to strangle for the trip when he heard shots coming from the house, and then the lord of the manor making his way to the barn, condemning everybody in earshot in the name of *Gott und der Teufel.* I'm quoting George; he's a sponge when it comes to tongues, foreign and otherwise. It's taken me fifty years to pick up as much English as he found in a month at Fort Lincoln.

He's fast afoot, too. He jumped down out of that loft while Drebber was coming in, ran to the house, through the open door, down the stairs, and into that ice box. The banging we heard was him trying to force open the door from inside—to defend himself if Drebber came back looking for him, or from anyone else, comes to that: Doing what he done to survive hadn't exactly taught him to expect rescue from strangers.

We got most of that out of him later. First we had to convince him we weren't there to finish what Drebber started, then run the bastard to ground before he had a chance to spread his good tidings among his neighbors.

The German boy that brung the news to town was gone, his mule too, so we followed Drebber's tracks, taking George along, since he knew the man and we didn't; what he might do, and to who first.

His footprints ended at a post sunk in the ground behind the house, where the boy said Drebber tethered his workhorse when he needed it handy; so it looked like that family squabble was a long time coming, and not what the newspapers call a "fit of hot blood," got up in the moment. He'd have had his escape route all mapped out before he took that rifle down from the wall. The trail led west—at a trot, based on the stride. He was so sure of himself he scorned to canter, much less gallop.

We got mounted, and without waiting for either of us to stick out a helping hand, George sprung up behind my cantle, slick as a frog. I might've expected him to choose Bremen's horse, pretty as it was, and my chestnut kind of patchy in the flanks, but when I pressed him later he said he preferred the American horse because the Arabian's nostrils were too big; after being shut up in that box he was jealous of the air it would take in. He denies saying it now, but judge for yourself: His name's not Mahomet.

Deputy Bremen's nose was reliable, damn every last hair inside it. That dull dead sky had opened up in two halves like a cracked egg and was dumping snow so fine and yet so thick that if you turned in the saddle to look back at the house and barn you had to take them on faith alone. The wind whipped them thousands of grains into your face and didn't let up, even after the face went dead as the face of a dried-up old king in a museum. You could hear them hit and it might have been someone else's face they was hitting.

The workhorse's tracks filled in as fast as the beast made them, and we couldn't see beyond our whiskers, or for that matter where the sky met the ground. It was like we were inside a porcelain bowl, surrounded by white, polished smooth, as if edges never existed. I was shouting at Bremen we might as well give up and hope to pick up a trail after the squall (choking on the snow that blew into my mouth and down my throat) when my horse shook itself and I knew my passenger had slid off. I thought he fell, but then the wind shifted, opening a second's gap in the curtain straight ahead, and I saw a skinny shape clouting forward through the drifts. To this day I don't know what he saw or how he saw it, but that boy was following a trail that didn't leave a trace an owl could make out with a spyglass. It's in his veins, I guess; away back when his God was making the world, a bloodhound got together with a turkey buzzard and out of that union popped his great-great-great-granddaddy.

A feature peculiar to that territory is a thing the natives call the "break in the plains," an escarpment starting east of the Missouri River and running at an angle clear to the border of Canada to the northwest, like a crack crossing a mirror corner to corner: A long time ago glaciers shoved a portion the size of New Hampshire up out of line, creating a step up from the low country to the Great Plains. Looking at a map you don't notice it so much, but crossing that line on horseback is like a bug climbing over the sharp edge of a paving stone; except no bug's dumb enough to try it in a blizzard. We humped our way up over that ridge by might and main: *might* being smacking our mounts' behinds with the ends of our reins, *main* being we practically had to step down and carry 'em on our backs; horses don't like the un-expected. And all the time the wind is pasting our brims against our crowns and throwing razor-ice into our eyes.

I reckon George had the worst of it, though: slogging through snow waist high, with the drifts smoothing everything over so you couldn't tell a rise or a dale from flat ground and the earth fell out from under you without warning and you dropped in over your head and had to claw your way back up into the air, gasping and blowing just the same as if you'd stumbled into a hole in a riverbed. But we never heard him complain.

It was slow going, and by the time the weather let up the fall of snow was turning purple starting in the east. We come in sight of a stand of box elder that some smart ploughman had planted in a row to make a windbreak along his western boundary. The drifts had piled up one side, leaving the ground level on the other, where smoke was rising in a thin thread from a little patch of orange that was a campfire.

Neither one of us had took along a glass, but there was a gray-brown mound near the fire, which George with his young eyes insisted was a bedroll and not a fallen tree limb.

"That's the son of a bitch!" Bremen snatched his carbine—it was a Spencer repeater—from its saddle scabbard and shouldered it. I leaned over and touched his arm and said, "We don't know he's *our* son of a bitch." I told the boy to sit tight, laid my Henry across my pommel and kneed my mare ahead.

We made about the same time following that shallow slope down to those trees as we had fighting our way through wind and snow, the hazards being equal. We were close enough to smell green wood burning when the chestnut put its foot in a chuckhole. It pitched left, corrected itself with a grunt, and I guess Bremen took that to mean I'd raked it with my spurs, because he raked his and charged down that grade, levering in a round with one hand and yelling like Johnny Reb; that's what snapping the tension will do to a cautious man, and thirty years later I can't bring myself to condemn him for it, as much as I cussed him at the time; and him a dead man.

Halfway to the trees he cartwheeled out of the saddle. His right foot hung up in the stirrup and he was drug for a yard or so before it twisted free, but I doubt he ever knew it, because when he stopped rolling he laid there like drip wax, twisted half onto his stomach, still holding that repeater flung out to the side.

Only then came the sound of the shot that took him, like the rifle had just remembered it's supposed to make noise. Just to make up for the delay it went on grumbling into the distance till a week from Sunday.

If Drebber had made a mistake—I mean apart from forgetting his better nature and slaughtering his wife and children over a disagreement of some sort—it was his choice of loads. A patch of that black-powder smoke could still be seen hanging around like a worn-out guest long after I drew rein, stepped down, bent one knee to the ground, and sent three rounds a third of the way up the trunk of the box elder the smoke was coming from. His rifle fell first, turning over once and coming to ground without a whisper, and then he came down on top of it, not nearly as quiet. I pumped a few more into him for luck, stood, and reloaded on the way down the slope, stopping long enough to turn Luther Bremen over and admire that clean shot through his heart. So the farmer was a good shot as well as a slippery eel, stuffing his bedroll with snow so it looked like he was asleep by the fire and climbing up a tree to wait for us to take the bait.

He'd come to light on his back with his arms splayed out, a snow angel with a red halo around his head, from a hole just down from the crown. But it would've been the slug that passed through both lungs that knocked him off his perch: It entered his chest on one side and passed out the other. He looked mean enough dead, with his eyes stuck out big as beer pulls from a face black with wrath, and a white scar running from one corner of his jaw to the temple opposite, like the break in the plains. I swung a boot at his side and heard something crack.

To hell with him. It could've been me just as easy, or both of us as we approached that campsite, riding slow. I had Luther Bremen to thank for my continued good health, offering himself up to the sacrifice even if he didn't plan it that way. But I don't suppose George Maledon blessed his memory for cheating him out of the hundred dollars he'd have charged to hang Drebber.

1926

Rawlings sat up straight; and unquestionably stiff. He was sitting at his rolltop in the waxen light of dawn with something stuck to the side of his face. He peeled away a loose page from his notebook and looked at it. Wild Bill Edwards spoke to him in the Pinkerton's own hand across a gulf of twenty years.

"Where's that plush private coach right now, you figure?"

Edwards had sounded wistful, but Rawlings never could determine when St. John's pet sharpshooter was laughing up his sleeve: His face, so spare of flesh anyone could see the muscles at work, pulled creases around the eyes behind the glasses and lifted the corners of his mouth; a purely collateral action. To the Pinkerton, those men who never showed humor and those who never showed anything else were equally unfathomable. Whenever this one spoke, his quadrangular chin slid sideways—"whopper-jawed" was the backwoods term—giving him the look of a sinister elf, his tongue buried in the off cheek.

The posse sat upright in a day coach belonging to the Denver & Rio Grande, which they'd boarded in Colorado Springs, letting their horses blow in the stock car. The change of transportation proved scant relief from saddlesores and exposure to the elements. It offered none of the amenities of the coach they'd abandoned in Elephant Crossing, on loan from the Southern Pacific; cinders from the locomotive stack twitched and crawled across the windows, leaving tracks like spiders scrambling through soot, and the sowbelly stove at the rear of the car struggled to keep up with winter in Colorado; and it wouldn't officially be winter for another two weeks.

The marshal took Edwards' question on face value. He'd left a crack in his window, allowing the suction to snatch away the smoke from his cigar; a gentlemanly gesture toward the civilians sharing the space.

"Right around Salt Lake City would be my guess; carrying some rich Mormon back home from sinful Denver, with a change to the Utah Central. He's taking a bath right now with as many of his harem as he can fit in that collapsible tub."

"Heathen swine."

Which was the first contribution Midian Pierce had made to the conversation since boarding—and a fair assessment of his own character, without the qualifier. As always, the professed evangelist sat across the aisle by himself, this time with the collaboration of all the other passengers. None seemed inclined to share accommodations with the smallish man in black, sounding out Scripture with such plosive actions of his lips that even a casual observer with a fair knowledge of

Holy Writ might identify the specific verse he was reading without looking at the text. The finger he dragged down each page was scrubbed clean and pink, the nail albumen-white, like a corpse's in a funeral parlor, the features of his face eerily ageless, as if preserved in paraffin, slick and dead. His threadbare Bible was bloated twice its original size by scraps of paper that stuck out from between the pages all around like ribbons: none, Rawlings noted, from the back half, commonly assigned to the New Testament. He suspected that some of Christ's mercy had been torn out to mark the sections Pierce favored. His was the God Who'd rolled dice with the Devil for Job's immortal soul.

George American Horse and the Mexicans were more isolated still, in sole possession of the seats in back. When the conductor had tried to deny them entry, insisting they ride with the freight, Rawlings had mollified him by peeling greenbacks from his expense roll—and prevented St. John and Edwards from pitching the railroad employee out onto the platform. The scene, and the nature of the party, accounted for the spare population of the coach on the busy morning run to Denver.

"Stretch out, boys," said Edwards. "Let the gentlefolk stand in the aisles next door if that's how they like it."

The pariahs made no response.

Indeed, George was unusually silent—surely not, on the evidence of his resigned behavior at the prospecting camp, merely because of the conductor's bigotry; he'd hardly be inclined to accept the surly Menéndezes as his misunderstood peers. He'd been quiet ever since St. John had told the ice box story. Rawlings wondered if the Indian was fuming over his loss of mystery, or whether he just didn't like to be talked about. Prior to then, all the Pinkerton had known of him was that he'd recently made his living play-acting the part of a hostile chief in Wild West exhibition traveling the gravel-road circuit; to which for some reason he couldn't return.

Rawlings redirected his attention to the marshal. "What makes you so certain we're still in pursuit of the Buckner gang and not pulling away from them? A train chasing a train is no kind of manhunt I ever heard of."

St. John's face crinkled in a tolerant smile. Unlike Wild Bill, he rarely dissembled his emotions.

"It's a new century, son; and the practice isn't so new at that. The armies down in Mexico have been fighting by rail since before Lincoln was shot. Maybe you Pinkertons think outlaws' horses don't wear out like everyone else's."

"Our information is this band caches fresh mounts in strategic locations along its line of retreat. That's how they manage to rob a bank in Denver and a train at Elephant Crossing only days apart. We can't blame faulty identification, with an amputated gunman present each time."

"And stash 'em like pirate gold all along the seven-hundred-mile road to Pinto Creek? Even ordinary horses don't come cheap, and famous bandits are obliged to pay a stiff tax to whoever helps out, for the risk; wranglers especially. Those round-muscled racers with deep bottoms draw notice like flies to sorghum, on top of which they ain't windfall you just pick up off the ground free for the stooping. To hear you tell it, Race and Merle are better off working for wages. Even Jim Shirley could find a position on a chicken ranch, biting peckers off roosters."

Edwards said, "Watch yourself, Cap'n. Rawlings might think you're calling him stupid and shoot you down like he done Joaquin."

"I never said it was Murietta I shot." Rawlings regretted his outburst instantly. He was only fueling his companions' suspicions. If he'd denounced the preposterous background the Agency had concocted for him at the start—but there was no profit in hindsight.

"Save it for the enemy, you two."

That rankled, and still did, and St. John twenty years in the grave. He'd treated them like squabbling siblings, scolded by a parent. If Edwards had shared Rawlings' resentment, his eternally humorous face didn't show it; and that was part of it as well, the smoldering grudge.

He pressed his thumb to his wrist. His pulse was galloping, but he left the tincture of coal oil in its pigeonhole in the desk and shuffled through his stack of fusty notebooks, Western Union envelopes, and hotel letterheads: distractions.

There had been a coda to the Drebber affair. St. John hadn't attached it to his account at the time, and Rawlings wasted a morning's work searching for it among his subsequent notes before he realized that the marshal had referred to it at least a week *before* he'd turned to his working holiday in Bismarck. The significance was missed because of the lack of context.

Sure enough, there it was, on page 3 of the very first entry in his history of what the hungry eastern press would refer to (in twenty-point type) as "The Last Manhunt of the Barbarous Days on the Border." He'd written it in St. Louis while he and St. John were awaiting replies to the marshal's wires to his old accomplices (and tentative posse): Smudged, stained, and torn, but laid out in neat stenographic-school characters in sepia ink from a hotel scratch pen, it read at first like an extinct legal squabble, imperfectly remembered thirty years after the fact. Now, transcribing it onto fresh sheets in the light of new intelligence, it became a comedy worthy of Shakespeare; or Molière at the least.

10

THE FARCE

But if anyone—aside from George American Horse—didn't waste tears over that snow angel, it was General Stephen Wheeler. He'd come to Fort Smith in '75 after serving with the First Michigan Volunteers at Pea Ridge and other places, and holding down assignments various and plenty in peacetime, to settle down finally as clerk in Parker's court. I knew him for the pinfeathers on his upper lip and chin and crippled right arm, the souvenir of a bullet fired by an unsuccessful assassin while he was working for the internal revenue; also his steel-shot eyes. A man of his parts and temperament wasn't like to welcome extra paperwork, however much it served justice, so extraditing a man from Dakota for killing a deputy sheriff and threatening the life of a federal officer wouldn't hold much appeal. Territorial authority is jealous of its homegrown assassins, and will hang them with local hemp, even if it means war with Washington.

Bremen's high-born horse wouldn't carry a corpse, so I lashed the two across the back of the claybank and led them up to where I'd left George, but all there was of him was tracks heading east. That was opposite the way back to Bismarck, so I didn't waste time following them, he not being my responsibility; anyway, he'd showed himself better equipped to deal with that country than I was, and if that blizzard should circle back, I'd need the boy I was looking for in order to pick up the trail to the boy I was looking for. You can see that didn't make sense.

Judge Parker was forced to postpone whatever penalty he had in store for that interview I gave J. Mercer Fleet, because I had to testify to a coroner's jury to determine the cause of Drebber's death. I don't recollect the name of the doctor who took the stand; he was part-time county coroner and full-time physician. He wasn't much older than me in spite of his fierce burnsides, but he wasn't likely to get much older than that, because he coughed a deal and kept looking at his handkerchief and didn't seem to like what he saw. Anyway he said he dug seven rounds out of Drebber, all but two of which would have settled his account. I was more concerned about the judge, who was named Flugelmann and a fellow Hasenpfeffer, but it come out that Drebber had been up before him three times for drunk and disorderly and assaulting Sheriff Yoder, for which last offense Flugelmann had sentenced him to ninety days, but suspended it as it was planting season and the defendant had a farm to run.

He was found to have met his fate through justified action by a peace officer; but before the gavel come down I asked if I was going to have to appear all over again in the case of Luther Bremen. The judge combed his whiskers over that, then allowed as how there was no need for an inquest in that case, the deputy having been slain by the deceased in the performance of his duty. But I wanted that on the record.

So you can imagine my surprise and consternation when two of Yoder's deputies stopped me at the door on the way out and arrested me for manslaughter.

Bremen's widow had decided to press charges, claiming I'd deliberately hung back from that campsite and was therefore responsible for what happened to her beloved husband. In her eyes I was a coward, and double-dealing to boot.

I will say the county jail was an improvement over that hole in Fort Smith. I had a cell to myself above ground with a high barred window letting in daylight, the necessary facilities were adequate, and though the grub wasn't anything to make the columns it didn't crawl away from you when you weren't looking. I was what Parker would call a "connoisseur" of the penal system in two countries, and Burleigh's met my approval, far as it went. Also I was fairly certain things would come out in my favor, as Yoder let me dictate a wire to Fort Smith and Old Thunder wasn't a man to mollycoddle murderers or their spouses the way his colleagues back East sometimes done.

Not that the situation made me a patient man. Communications weren't what they are now in the age of Mr. Bell's invention, and Parker had his hands in cess up to his elbows attending to real criminals. So I sat and stewed and brooded over my sins. I reckon it was that Dakota experience that satisfied my curiosity as to the wonderments of the frontier. I'd have settled for that sinkhole I drunk in last year over my circumstances at the time.

Olive Bremen come to look at me through the bars. Her kind's a lot more common now out here: a latecoming pilgrim accustomed to the virtues of civilization while possessing nothing of what it takes to bring it about; all whalebone and feathers and New Jersey indignation. I don't say she wasn't attractive. She was younger than her husband, who'd have made two of her in flesh alone, and I'm partial to high color in a woman. I couldn't blame Bremen for his choice, though I can't think what she saw in him as a candidate for high office, impetuous as he was. She held the position of recording

secretary with the G.A.R., her father having fit under Rose-
crans at Murfreesboro, then made his fortune in flax after
Sherman burnt all the cotton fields down South. She was a
founding member of the Bismarck Ladies' League for City
Betterment and I guess other things as well, as suited a future
First Lady of Dakota. Though she didn't speak a word to me,
if eyes was cannons there'd have been nothing to mark my
visit to her town but a smoking hole in the brick wall behind
me. Anyway, when she was finished she flounced on out to
write another letter to *The Dakotan* demanding law enforce-
ment reform and my head on a trencher.

Believe it or not, I saw her side of the affair. She'd counted
on living in the capital someday, hosting presidents and
princes and lording it over all the wives of mere attorney generals, and now would have to start all over from scratch. Some
folks—not just women, but them oftener than men—feel the
need to flush all the disappointment out of their systems before they can turn their hand to practical matters. You can't
concentrate on rebuilding your house while you're passing a
gallstone. The gallstone in this case being me.

Three weeks into my incarceration, a party of Deputy
U.S. Marshals met with Sheriff Yoder, having come straight
to his office in the courthouse from the Fort Smith train,
still sooty from the journey, bringing with them the assistant prosecuting attorney for the Western District of Arkansas with a writ wrote in Latin calling for my carcass to
be brought forth into his care; which Yoder was only too
pleased to respect. He'd had his ears pinned back by the Ladies' League till they was too tight to his head to hook his
spectacles over them, and mad as a scalded badger over the
injustice to the man who'd taken away his deputy's killer
and all-around splinter-in-the-ass of his jurisdiction besides,

and fed up with being tied down in his service to the community by a carpet-bagging widow from Bayonne.

Yoder didn't much care for the letter Parker had sent with the party, accusing him of "perpetrating a farce that can only contribute to the destruction of law and order on the frontier" (and dispatched a copy to President Hayes), but I guess he was too relieved to get up on his hind legs, and Judge Flugelmann agreed. My old friend Royal Ames was along on that expedition: He quoted the sheriff on that carpet-bagging remark word for word.

It all worked out for me, because instead of taking away my star for sharing federal business with everyone who had a dime to spare for Frank Leslie's paper, Parker satisfied his choler with a stern lecture and these parting words: "Now go forth from my presence, 'Swami Ike,' and sin no more where I can hear you."

And there was a smile half-hid in those gray whiskers: God smite me to ashes if there wasn't.

1926

The ten-foot cabinet clock in Mrs. Balfour's foyer struck one; the gong, deep and oratorical, paused inside his skull to resonate between the ears, then passed on. He laid down his pen and reached for his watch, but his fingers were crabbed like garden claws and wouldn't go into the pocket. He flexed them—squeezing an imaginary rubber ball—got some feeling into the knuckles, and fished it out by its chain: 1:31 A.M. The clock had bonged that single note three times in succession.

He unfolded himself from his chair, one joint at a time, like erecting a tent; arched his back, hands on hips, got a chorus of crackles, and crossed to the washbasin. His right leg had gone to sleep: The foot was wrapped in ten layers of cotton for all it felt of the floor. Blood rushed back into it, burning. He filled the basin from the pitcher, rolled up his shirtsleeves, cupped his hands, splashed tepid water into his face and let it stream off his chin for a moment before hooking the towel off its wooden spindle.

He wrenched up the window and thrust his head into the damp air. The street below, lonely even at the height of the commute, was at its most isolated at that hour. A solitary Model T Opera Coupe—a tall, awkward box on wheels— ticked its way from one streetlit corner to the next, towed by twin cones of light from its headlamps; instead of interrupting the loneliness, it confirmed it. A locomotive pulled its chortling length of cars through a crossing six blocks east, trailing its whistle; a coal-burner. His ears were abnormally acute: He could distinguish between the measured beat of a woodburning engine and the asthmatic cough of one fueled by anthracite or bitumen; although he was prepared to concede he was influenced by the association with black lung.

He turned away, leaving the window open, and looked at the pile of foolscap on the desk, the top sheet curling inward at the corners toward the ink bottle he used for a paperweight. In less than a week he'd managed to exhume nearly a hundred pages in longhand from schoolboy characters scribbled mostly from memory, when St. John wasn't actually engaged in anecdote; Rawlings had had to retire to a corner to commit it to paper. To be caught setting down a man's casual reminiscences defeated the purpose, like observing a wild animal in captivity: The animal changed its behavior, the man stopped recollecting. If Rawlings' field position were to be permanent (which in those days had seemed important), he needed to understand men like the marshal. That meant recording his every utterance as if it were the Gospel According to St. John.

He was a gifted storyteller, although certainly not a scrupulously accurate one; his biographer, who'd studied his case before approaching him in St. Louis with Pinkerton's offer, noticed discrepancies in dates and the order of events. (The pursuit of Bob Squire and Clara Hornbeck had not been continuous, as he'd reported. The trail had gone cold for weeks in the middle, during which he and Ames were dispatched to Muskogee to arrest a whiskey smuggler; and he'd testified at Sam Crosstree's trial not in December 1876, but a month later, in January 1877.) But Rawlings' brief acquaintance with Buck Jones—and a research visit to a Rochester theater showing one of his western features—had convinced him that historical detail had less to do with fiscal success in Hollywood than horseback chases and gunplay, regardless of whether they had anything to do with the story. (The comely Rose Blossom, he felt, would please audiences as Jenny Umber, even though "poor Jenny" was dead before the marshal entered the picture; pert creatures in ringlets had changed the concept of feminine beauty since the days of Wardle's Cosmograph.)

St. John wasn't a reader. He passed the time spinning tales, seldom at great length and even less often in direct connection with one another, but always (or so it appeared) to his listeners' interest.

The others eluded boredom in their own ways. George divided his time while aboard train between books—the late lamented private coach had come equipped with a moderately well-stocked library, and his mission-school education seemed to have left him with tastes running from Browning to Fenimore Cooper—and visits to the vestibule to spare his companions the ordeal of the nasty black cheroots he bought in towns along the way. (The fouler the merchandise, it seemed, the more inexhaustible the supply.) Edwards napped and prowled through newspapers, the wire columns mostly, Pierce had his psalms and parables, and Rawlings his travel journals; St. John had concluded that he was keeping track of expenses for the bookkeepers in Chicago, and Rawlings let him.

A chill puff of air through the open window in his boarding house room made him shudder; his doctor had admonished him against loitering in drafts. He shoved the sash down and returned to the desk, to mount a fresh expedition through the lopsided stack of notebooks.

Something about the cold.

There it was:

"He said it was cold weather saved you."

The comment belonged to George American Horse, not St. John; that's why it had eluded him so long. He was in the habit of skimming through the penciled paragraphs, often illegible or half-erased by time and the irregular quality of the graphite available in prairie towns, searching for the symbol belonging to the marshal's name, when any contribution from so long an associate as the Indian was worth a second look.

But there had been an interruption; a rockslide across the tracks, or some fresh intelligence regarding the Buckners at a water stop, and he had to shuttle back and forth through the stack to find where the narrative had picked up.

George: "Ten degrees warmer, the doc said, and you'd have bled white halfway to Fort Smith. Cold slowed the circulation."

St. John: "And if that bullet had been rimfire instead of

centerfire it would've smashed itself flat against my hip-
bone and you'd have plucked it out with your fingers and
I wouldn't still feel it every time it rains. How things might
have went and how they went's got as much to do with each
other as pigsties and penguins."

11

PHEASANT'S BLUFF

I been shot three times: Once through the gut, another time in the second toe of my right foot, then again in the flesh of my left calf; or was it the right? I disremember, but it was years later, when I was a public safety officer in Turkey Creek. That first one afflicts me still—the bullet played out next to my spine, which is where the rheumatism settled—but I regret that toe most, because every time I tug off my boots and see the stump, I get to missing Royal Ames all over again.

Folks who was there have called me out betimes for mixing up my years, but you don't have to ask me twice to fix on March 28, 1886, as the day I lost my friend.

I'd just turned thirty, after ten years in the Nations, which is when most men in my profession contemplate retirement while it's still our decision. Hickok got his permanent ticket-of-leave at thirty-nine, and Earp told me he was constipated for life after that business in Arizona when he was thirty-three, which may explain why he was such a miserable son of a bitch to get along with. Still is.

I'd been behaving myself long enough the Judge offered to recommend me to President Cleveland for appointment to U.S. Marshal; he was short one at the time and impatient of a replacement. I slept on it. It was a desk job, oftenest filled by generals and former judges, and once you've spent a month on your back after a country doctor unscrewed a hunk of metal from your insides wrong way out, the occasional paper-cut is no hardship.

But before he could decide whether to write that letter, the President got off the stick and named someone else to the position. Not having money in the bank nor even the acquaintance of one, I put aside my reservations as to the hazards and oiled my saddle. I'd traded the chestnut, which was too old to cut trail but still good for hauling a cart, along with some cash, for a fine roan gelding: It was retired from General Miles's cavalry, where it lost any bashful attitude it might have entertained toward the noise of gunfire and the stink of powder and blood, and was tame enough not to try and bite a chunk out of my ass every time I leaned back on the cinch. I called it Geronimo.

Ames, just before he left on the east central circuit, joshed me about that U.S. Marshal deal.

"You didn't want it anyway, Ike," he said. "You don't have the whiskers for the position; the belly neither, with your approach to victuals. I once saw you eat a rotten egg, and compliment the cook after." Well, it's true that jail fare in Mexico and that pisshole in Fort Smith hadn't inclined me toward the sin of gluttony, but I threw my bridle at him for the remark. If I'd known it was the last time I'd see him I'd have made it evening primrose. I hadn't exactly lied when I told Mercer about my gift for seeing around corners, but it played me false that time.

Fergus Glass, an army deserter taken up with a Choctaw woman, was accused of stealing a horse, which was a capital crime then, the want of a mount being a common cause of death from exposure to heat, cold, and scavengers, and surrendered himself into Ames's custody without a squawk, him being yellow like most runagates of the type; but he had friends—or if they wasn't exactly that, they were at least enemies of everything pinned to a badge, which amounted to the same thing. Dick Spanish was one. He laid in wait along the Rattlesnake Mountain road with a Colt revolving rifle and shot Ames through the neck as he rode past, with Glass riding alongside, tied wrists and ankles aboard the horse he stole, which was Ames's preferred method for transporting criminals; as well I remembered, having rid my old chestnut the same way after the quarrel with LeFever. Spanish cut Glass loose and they "rode hurriedly away," according to court records, but not in such a rush they didn't stop to separate the dead man from his watch, an old-fashioned piece that had belonged to his father, a Negro freedman married to an Osage, who was Royal's mother. It was evidence in Glass's trial later, with the initials "R.A." scratched inside the case by Ames himself.

Glass's accomplice may not have noticed the theft. He was smart enough to leave Ames's horse behind, not wanting to call attention to himself aboard a good Fort Smith mount; but that watch was enough to hang them both.

Spanish—whose name wasn't Spanish, but Seaton, having rechristened himself for Spaniard Creek, where he was born near Muskogee—might have got away with it, too, if he wasn't betrayed by his own dog. (A clever scrivener with *The Fort Smith Elevator* named it "General Arnold," after Benedict of lasting dishonor, though my own assessment of the animal's character is more charitable.)

You probably wouldn't know that dog from any of the yellow mongrels you see stretched out in the middle of the road, dead or stupefied by heat, green flies bunched like grapes in the wet of their eyes; but folks that knew Spanish recognized his dog by a missing ear-tip and a white spot on its nose like it mistook a hot iron for a canine associate's butt. It followed Spanish around when it felt like it, and he kicked it the way a man licks his wife and not his neighbor's; apart from that, the locals wouldn't swear that either party was committed to the relationship. The dog knew where the man threw out the kitchen slops, and the man found the dog convenient to spit on when he'd just swept the floor. But that dog was at Pheasant's Bluff that day, and was an eyewitness to the event. It was still laying there with its chin resting on Ames's leg when a fellow out gigging frogs come along and recognized it. "Spanish's dog," he told the postmaster in town. "Though it looks like it made up its mind to switch."

"Leetle late," said the postmaster, and sent his boy to the Lighthorse Police, Spanish being half-Cherokee and subject to their authority.

The police boxed up Ames's remains and escorted them to Fort Smith for burial; one of twenty-five federal officers murdered before Oklahoma got its star on the flag. Remember that next time someone tells you Parker was rope-crazy.

The Judge took it personal. As set as he was on protecting the people in his care from brigands and blacklegs, when one of 'em took the life of a marshal, it was Katy bar the door. He posted a reward of five hundred dollars for Spanish and Glass each and put together a hunting party with orders to turn the territory wrongside out if we had to, but bring in Spanish, alive if possible for judgment, but in any case brung in. I stood up first, and five more come after right quick. Some I knew well, like Joe Sky, some not at all, others to speak to, including one who wouldn't speak back: Heck Thomas was a straight-arrow that knew my history and was always waiting for me to turn coat again and run up the Jolly Roger; but he knew too I was tight with Royal, so he kept his own council as to his thoughts on the matter, as I weren't likely to crawfish on that particular assignment.

Glass, it was known, shared a cabin with his Choctaw squaw on the Canadian, but when we got there to search the place she had her girl fetch a Bible and laid her hand on it and swore she hadn't seen him in a month. She was pious, a volunteer at the First Baptist when pox broke out and the elders turned the church into an infirmary, so we accepted it; although Joe Sky holding a Bowie to her girl's throat helped in the decision. She was a niece or something. The woman said Glass sometimes traded at McAlester's store, which in the Choctaw meant selling whiskey.

McAlester and his wife were a reliable source of information on what went on in the Choctaw, so we turned a blind eye to the things they sold out of the back of the store. That made ours a friendly visit.

We tied up behind the store, on the theory that someone who dropped by for beans and coffee might spot six well-toned horses at the rail in front, make the connection, and carry the tale. Mrs. McAlester was behind the counter, and was talking to Heck Thomas when someone came in through the front door.

She said, "Will that be all, Mr. Turnbull?"

That was a sign intended for the marshals; Turnbull was a popular brand of men's collar then, and a sly reference to the neckware Maledon fit to his customers. The Judge didn't care for it, not being partial to levity of that sort, but by the time he got wind there wasn't time to change it so it would get around to folks we trusted, so he let it stand. It was one we all knew, and Fergus Glass found himself in the middle of a half-circle field of fire with his hands high and his face white as pigeon shit behind the grime: He'd been sleeping in barns and haystacks for weeks, eating raw eggs he stole from chicken coops, with his overalls torn and hanging by one strap. We found out later he'd parted company with Dick Spanish, not caring to be caught in the company of a man who'd killed a marshal. (Spanish in his turn took Glass's stole horse in trade for not making him the good-bye gift of a bullet.) He was a sorry sight.

He was unarmed but for the clasp knife we took from him, along with Ames's watch. That scared him into confessing, without the encouragement we'd normally have employed. He said he'd come to the store hoping to strike a bargain: a barrel of whiskey (when he had it) in return for a place to burrow in: A desperate act, considering the profit to be made from turning down the offer and giving him up for the reward, but he didn't have any other security to put up. He told us Spanish was headed for the Wildhorse range up on the Arkansas. We put Glass in charge of the Choctaw Police and headed that direction.

There was an old ice house up that way, a sturdy log building, double-sheathed and insulated with sawdust, with a fallen-in roof. Joe Sky was familiar with it: It was a favorite stopping-place for those weary travelers who found boarding houses too conspicuous, and the closest thing in those parts you'd find to a fort. We approached it from the back, where someone had built on a lean-to with boughs and tar-paper from what was left of the roof. Two horses were tethered inside, blowing hard and flecked with lather.

We strung a picket line for the horses down the bank from the cabin and surrounded the place: two men in back, two in front, and one on either side, with rifles and carbines. One of the marshals—White was his name, his face was new to me—had lungs made of leather and bound with brass, so it was him that bawled out:

"Show yourself, Dick! There's marshals on all sides, and we want to go home!"

Well, anyone knew what that meant. In spite of those fortifications, it wasn't going to be no all-day, all-night siege like what it took to flush out Ned Christie years later; not if we had anything to say about it. That one's in the history books, but we wasn't any of us interested in making history that day. Everyone liked Ames.

I'm not sure what happens to time in that situation; whether Spanish wasn't expecting us and took a moment to collect himself, or whether it was just a second, and the lag was all in our heads. It seemed to me I could've went out, got a haircut, and been back before the answer came.

Then come the bang. Smoke squirted out of the building just above ground level and then White went down with a shattered ankle.

That was our fault. There was a big barn door for carrying in the ice, fixed up on a slide and open a couple of inches, and we expected the answer to come from there; but it never pays to doubt the cards in a man's hands or how he plays them. Spanish had poked a hole in the chinking between the bottom log and the stone foundation, just big enough to make a gun port, and White paid for our mistake with a limp for life.

Then everything happened at once. We opened fire all around, knocking bark off the logs in sheets and exposing yellow underneath, with a racket like six riverboats blowing their boilers one after the other in a chain. Bitter smoke rose to the treetops and clung there like it was spun by webworms; it stung our eyes and blocked our throats, but we

kept on firing and reloading. We was all down on our stom-
achs by then, White drug back from where he fell by two
other deputies; and credit unto him, because he was shooting and pumping in fresh cartridges and shooting again right
along with the rest of us. Spanish returned fire, first from
this end of the cabin, now from the other, then from points
in between, the slugs chugging into the ground close enough
to throw dirt up your nose. There was a lot more than one
hole in that chinking, and he was generous in how he made
use of them, scrambling all around the floor to shoot at the
men on all sides. Wearing holes in the knees of his britches.

But he was just one man, and couldn't be everywhere at
once. When bullets stopped coming our direction and we
heard the muffled sound of the shots from in back, Thomas
gave me and Joe Sky the signal, and we run up to the front,
snatching up armloads of creosote and juniper by the roots,
bunching 'em up against the foundation, and touching them
off while the others knocked more kindling off the building
up high to give cover. The men stationed at the sides and
back were to do the same thing when Spanish turned his attention away from them.

That dry brush went up like fireworks. Flames licked at
the logs and threw towers of sparks up columns of smoke that
must've been seen as far away as Fort Smith. The fire caught
all around, and as it climbed higher than the house it looked
like Spanish had made the decision to go up with it, which
met with our approval, since we wouldn't be present to
watch him burning in hell. But if that was his intention he'd
changed his mind, because that door slid all the way to the
end of its track with a bang and he come charging out, yelling and spitting bullets from the revolving rifle he'd used
to kill Ames; and didn't he make a fine target, with them

flames lighting him up from behind, and him a dark man, with black hair and beard and big black checks on his shirt so we could each pick one to draw a bead on, like a bottle on a fencerail?

We tore up that shirt to bind White's ankle, which is why Spanish is wearing just his ripped britches and flannel underwear and boots in the only picture he ever posed for, with seventeen holes in him; which was a record at the time.

It wasn't my idea, that picture. I was taking a dally around his ankles, fixing to drag him up and down the Choctaw Nation from horseback till the back of his head stopped making noise on the ground, but Thomas overruled me. So we took him to Muskogee and stood up a trestle table in front of the barbershop with him leaning against it and a photographer that had a studio there took his picture with his arms folded at his waist holding his rifle. I saw that photograph for sale a few months ago, on a cabinet card in a train station in Albuquerque: a trophy, like a moose head or a planked trout. I don't see that's any better than what I had in mind for him.

That didn't help my case with Heck Thomas. He never got past the notion my reckless youth would catch up with me someday. He come up to me in Council Bluffs when I was drumming up votes on a platform in front of the town hall. His moustaches was gray as dust and his neck hung down in wattles, but his eyes was still bright, like fireflies in a jar. His hand came up and I stuck mine out; I guess I'll never learn, because he didn't take it. He pointed his finger at me, said, "I knew it!" and walked away.

III

THE LAST MANHUNT

1

MR. KENNEDY

Joseph P. Kennedy slid something from a softly shining briefcase, set the case on the floor beside his chair, and thrust the object across the table. Rawlings recognized the homely brown cardboard portfolio he'd mailed to Buck Jones in California three weeks ago, tied with a string. He took it and laid it in his lap.

"You're rejecting it."

He analyzed the tone of his own voice: disappointment or relief? Certainly it released him from a doubtful obligation; on a more personal level, the five hundred dollars he'd banked in advance of delivery was suffering from erosion. His pension from the Agency barely covered his rent.

The businessman from Boston sat unblinking behind the round lenses of his spectacles; he seemed to have no lids. A trim man in his late thirties, with the skim-milk complexion of the true redhead and hair plastered back from a high broad brow, he wore a charcoal double-breasted suit cut to his measure and a diagonally striped tie, the stripes alternating between broad and narrow. His hands were well-kept, but with thick veins on the backs that looked to have been molded from clay; behind the lace-curtain Irish was a long chain of bricklayers and tenant farmers. The Agency manual trained Pinkerton detectives to pay attention to such things as hands.

"Rawlings. That's English, isn't it?"

Was it imagination, or was there a touch of brogue in the question that hadn't been apparent before; a challenge excavated from some ancient field of battle? Hard to tell under the broad vowels and emphatic *r*'s of Bunker Hill.

"I suppose it is. I haven't researched it. I was born in Ohio and so were both my parents."

"Indiana, me," said Buck Jones. "We were practically neighbors." The cowboy star chuckled as if he'd made some kind of point; his nervousness was palpable.

With good reason. The restaurant he'd chosen, on Seventh Street in Minneapolis, was a mistake. The shamrock motif was subtle—woven into the linens, white on white—but the subliminal effect was plain as a clay pipe. The fare was worse: corned beef, cabbage, boiled redskin potatoes, and an extensive selection of Irish whiskies (the last not on the menu, but alluded to discreetly by their waiter). Although the patrons dressed conservatively, they tucked their napkins inside their collars, and the ambient conversation rose and fell with the lilt of County Cork. Kennedy ordered the halibut. "Scotch," he added, handing back the menu.

Rawlings wondered if the restaurant's stock had been supplied by Kennedy himself. He'd looked up Jones's benefactor in the newspaper room of the Rochester library: railroads, shipping, stocks and bonds; bootlegging. A man who'd tamed the federal anti-trust laws would brush off Coast Guard patrols without breaking a sweat. Rawlings was a detective, after all.

The exchanges during dinner had been general: Kennedy's train ride from Boston was uneventful; Jones's from Los Angeles had been interrupted by a faulty switch in New Mexico; the Massachusetts weather was sunny when left behind, in California rainy; the Kennedy children were "fat as stoats"; Jones's stunt double on the set of *The Gentle Cyclone* had gotten into a real-life fistfight with Will Walling; Rawlings was well, thank you.

The portfolio changed hands over coffee. If this was rejection, it was at least delivered in person, and not in a chilly wire from the Pinkerton's chief counsel.

"Not a rejection," Kennedy said, in response to his comment; "not at all. Not yet, anyway. I'm suggesting you take another look at it."

"What would I be looking for?"

"The structure is episodic. We're not discussing a Saturday-afternoon serial laid out in quarter-hour chapters spread out over ten weeks. Seventy-nine minutes is the standard running time; much more, and the audience gets restless. And we cannot have talk of hard-ons and whores." Did the man blush? His fair skin was the only thing about him that seemed transparent.

"I'm aware of that. It was necessary for me to set down St. John's speech as I heard it, in order to recapture the experience. Any publisher would edit out the questionable material, and I assumed whoever wrote the title cards for the scenario would do the same. As to the structure—"

"Scenarists are lazy, and the public has grown astute. Paramount had to reshoot most of a major feature last year after audiences read the actors' lips during the premiere and made complaints. There's entirely too much drinking done on those stages."

No blush this time, but the remark seemed hypocritical, if not priggish; doubtless some of the drink carried Kennedy's label.

He pushed on, as if he was aware of the irony. "As to the structure. It's one anecdote after another, colorful but unrelated; more suitable to a barbershop than a theater at ten cents the seat."

"The assignment was to write St. John's life story. What is that, if not a series of anecdotes?"

"So it is; but it's only *half* the story. Where is the Buckner Gang? *The Last Manhunt* is the working title."

A vacuum of silence settled around their table. The actor cleared his throat; he'd caught Rawlings' accusing eye.

"It occurred to me when you sent me one of those old press cuttings," he said. "I liked the sound of it. *The Iron Star* seemed—well, *The Iron Horse* was a big hit for Fox; I thought the reviewers might accuse us of trying to cash in on its success and fail to give it a fair hearing. And then there's Fox himself; we'll be in competition with him when we form a new production company."

If Kennedy decides to sponsor it, Rawlings thought. So far the man had given no indication he was seriously considering partnering with Jones. The money that had changed hands meant nothing: Financiers of his description handed out five-hundred-dollar checks the way they tipped railway porters, and transected the country as casually as crossing the street. More than possibly he had an appointment that week with W. R. Hearst at San Simeon, or some other satrap on the West Coast, and this was just a stopover.

"Let me worry about men like Fox," Kennedy said. (Rawlings glimpsed the word *Jews* gliding like a fish just below the surface of "men like Fox.") "The time and its setting appeals. Based on what I've seen, most western films are stuck between the Civil War and the century's turn, so this would set it apart. And there's a definite advantage in recreating a period only twenty years in the past. Good Lord, there were *automobiles* then! Rockefeller has an Edison up on blocks he wanted to donate to the Smithsonian and deduct it from the income tax. They turned him down, but I'm on the board of several charitable— Yes, Mr. Jones?"

Spectacles or not, his peripheral vision was excellent. Jones was scowling down at his cup. He looked up.

"There are no automobiles in westerns."

"Indeed? Well, no doubt you're better informed. John D. can manage without my help." Kennedy pointed at the portfolio in Rawlings' lap. "We can address that old material in flashback. The relative youth of the fugitives in this"—he groped for a phrase—"this *swan song,* might draw in female audiences. Women are drawn to rogues. As a matter of fact, that strapping young fellow in *The Iron Horse* would make an ideal Race Buckner. Well, Mr. Rawlings?"

"I haven't seen the film."

"We're discussing your story. As I understand it, you were actually present on the manhunt; that's what attracted me to this endeavor. Why not give us the benefit of personal experience, instead of repeating the hoary reminiscences of an old man?"

Rawlings was the same age St. John was then; but he ignored the slight. "There are obstacles in that path."

"There always are. Tell us what they are, and we'll address them."

His pulse was elevated—not from vexation, but from the pleasurable anticipation of pricking the balloon of this modern-day robber baron; this jumped-up shanty Mick in a suit tailored for a gentleman.

"To begin with, the manhunt was a failure."

Address that.

* * *

Without pausing to shed his coat and hat, Rawlings filled a glass from the pitcher on the basin in his room, put in two drops from the bottle of tincture, and drank it in one long draught, standing up. Then he took his seat at the desk. It was late; he'd caught the last train from Minneapolis. That made him sole witness to all the contented sounds an old house makes when its occupants have gone to bed.

The hem of his coat sagged to one side under the weight in the saddle pocket, pooling on the floor. He excavated the portfolio and flung it onto the desk. His fountain pen jumped out of its groove on the inkstand and rolled to the edge of the blotter.

A rectangle of paper, dislodged from the pocket along with its lining, drifted down to the planks at his feet. From that distance the angular signature at the bottom looked like a series of exclamation points—an illusion, because the Kennedys of this world never had to emphasize or underscore or raise their voices above a whisper.

It was a reprieve, granted as a symbol of confidence that the Bostonian's wishes would be honored; or would for at least as long as two hundred fifty dollars held out.

The check was perforated on three sides, torn from a book the size of a ledger. He would have made it out, added his flourish, unzipped it, set it aside, and proceeded to the next, like a baker cutting cookies from a sheet of dough. (Was that the origin of the vulgarism?) All arguments had thus been answered, probably before he left Boston.

A failure, Mr. Rawlings? In life, perhaps; but this isn't life, is it? And who is around to call you out for tampering with the details after the fact: Race Buckner? "Dead or alive," as the posters used to say? If he is alive, and is as wily as his press, he will hardly come out of hiding to straighten out the record.

Lives were taken, and are bound to be laid at his feet, whether or not it was his finger on the trigger.

Lives were taken, yes.

How odd, Rawlings thought, when they were discussing Buck Jones's movie, that Kennedy should have brought up the subject of automobiles.

2

MERCURY CITY

"George, you're standing. Pull the cord."

The Indian, a restless soul, spent more time in the aisle than in a seat. He glanced from St. John to the cable running the length of the car just under the roof; reached up and gave it a sharp tug.

The handful of civilian passengers in the car felt the lurch and clutched at the seats in front of them to keep from colliding with the frames. Apart from that there was no significant disturbance: Each segment of the train responded in chain reaction according to the Westinghouse system, with a brief delay in between. The brakes exhaled a blast of air, the wheels shrieked against the rails, steel on steel, the car rocked forward, then back, and slid to a gentle stop. By that time the party was on its feet, hoisting bedrolls and carbines down from the luggage shelves overhead.

Rawlings was last. "We're leaving the train? Why?"

"'Swami Ike,'" muttered Edwards, strapping his gun belt around his narrow waist. "That son of a bitch Parker's got a lot to answer for. I'd shoot him dead if he wasn't already."

They had stopped where the tracks crossed a trail: two ruts carved ankle-deep in the snow-covered grass by generations of prairie schooners, and before them the travois of nomadic tribes following the path of the buffalo. The horses picked their way unsteadily down the ramp from the stock car and paused at the bottom to blow straw dust from their nostrils, tossing their heads and rippling their withers like dogs shaking themselves dry. Edwards paused, holding his saddle in both hands, to watch the caboose shrivel into the distance. The smoke from the engine lingered with its smell of sweet cedar and bitter dogwood.

"We sure spend a lot of time staring at the ass-end of trains," he said. "When this is over I mean to buy a ticket on a sleeper in Frisco and ride clear to Brooklyn without ever stepping off."

George smirked. "What do you know about Brooklyn?"

"Only everything up to when I ran away at twelve."

"I thought you were from Texas."

"I made my stake shooting rustlers. Try telling a cattleman in that fix you're from Flatbush and see where it gets you."

"We're all of us Easterners," St. John said. "Except you, George, and the Menéndezes. I don't know about Rawlings beyond Cheyenne."

"Cincinnati," he said, before the conversation could move any further in that direction.

"See? Everybody out here came from someplace else. Not counting Mexicans and Indians."

The Mexicans, who had lifted their heads when their name was spoken, said something in their mongrel tongue, a mix of Spanish, Indian, and some kind of oral shorthand common to vagabonds. St. John responded in the same, at length.

Edwards said, "Boys, I got a hunch the muchachos know more about where we're headed than us Americans."

St. John secured his bedroll behind his cantle and slid his

Henry into it. "They asked. You didn't. I know this crossing. You wouldn't think it now, but there was a wide-open town here once: Mercury City. The locals took it all apart when the U.P. moved on—saloon, store, bank, whorehouse, and churches; two of 'em, Presbyterian and Methodist, which is civilization for you—loaded it on wagons, and put it all back together at the next end of track. I was there for the show: every nail, peg, hasp and staple took out and packed in crates with labels on 'em. I think that's where Cody got the idea for his traveling exhibition. There was a farmers' co-op, and dugouts spread out half a day's ride east. I don't guess them grangers raised much more than blisters, but there might still be some soddies standing. If I was an outlaw headed up Wyoming way I'd be tempted to lay over for a night."

"Why here especially?" Rawlings said. "There must be dozens more places just like it. Oh."

The others, all but the Mexicans, had turned to look at him. He flushed—from anger, not embarrassment. Not only had the vain old bird fallen prey to his own press; he'd managed to drag the others into his delusion.

Pierce spoke up, breaking the spell. He hadn't uttered a word for hours that didn't come from the Good Book. "What would bring a man of your character to expose himself to so many eyes?"

St. John, the politician, ignored the slight. "Hauling freight: Pipes and well points, that trip. It was between raiding and marshaling, when I couldn't find honest work."

"You are lost to redemption."

"That's been said."

Rawlings studied the prim little man in his flat-brimmed hat and cutaway coat buttoned to the neck, cinerary black against the snow: a lower-case *t* torn from a black-letter Bible.

What could possibly have made him curious about St. John's business in the extinct community of Mercury City? Was there shared history there? Apart from his tenure in the Nations—which was transient work in itself—the marshal had spent his life in perpetual motion, either in flight from past indiscretions or in search of the next billet (brigandry, muleskinning, keeping the peace: all occupations that could be picked up and set back down with a minimum of exertion). There was something of the Bedouin in the Sunday school teacher as well; a true evangelist might break character now and then, but not Midian Pierce. He was too authentic to accept at face value, and too arrogant to see it.

St. John shielded his eyes against the sun. "Dark won't wait on us. Let's go exploring."

The horses churned through fresh drifts, their breath smoking in the cold. The light was growing mellow when they stopped on the crest of a ridge and looked down on a long single-story building with a stone chimney built against an end wall. It had no windows and a covered porch leaned away from the front of the structure with a violent twist to its frame, as if a titan had taken it in both hands and wrenched it in two directions. Firs had sprung up around it, obstructing the path to the steps. A tin weathervane, twisted similarly, clung to the peak of the roof.

"That'd be the old farmers' cooperative," St. John said. "George?"

"Any tracks are wearing a foot and a half of snow. There weren't any to begin with would be my guess."

"You always was a better tracker than a guesser. Bill?"

"I never seen a place more empty. If I was a ghost I wouldn't bother to haunt it."

Rawlings didn't wait for an invitation. "Your crystal ball's got a crack in it, Marshal. No one's been here since they took away the town."

"Fine lot of manhunters. Look at the roof."

He looked. It was swaybacked, the shingles overgrown with moss from the shade of the firs. "It's about to fall in."

"Look again."

"What am I looking for?"

"Something that ain't there."

"Snow," George said.

"Good. There was a fire inside, melting it off; and not last week." As if to confirm the statement, his claybank shifted its weight. The fresh fall creaked beneath the pressure.

"We might catch up to them between here and Pinto Creek."

"First things first, George. Mebbe the fire died out and they're still inside asleep."

"'There is no peace,'" said Pierce, "'unto the wicked.'"

Edwards said, "There's no horses neither."

"Picketed out back," said St. John; "or inside handy, the way Bonney done it. This bunch steals from the best." He drew a brass-cased spyglass from his saddlebag, unfolded it, and trained it on the building. After a moment he reached the glass across to Rawlings.

"Your eyes are younger than mine. Is that a rooster?"

The Pinkerton focused on the weathervane.

"A bear, I think. Possibly a raccoon."

George said, "You're both blind. It's a buffalo."

St. John put away the glass. "Bill, cut us a steak off the hump."

Edwards, the sharpshooter, unscabbarded his rifle, a Remington rolling-block with a range of five hundred yards, and swung out of the stirrups; the snow was so deep Rawlings wouldn't have been surprised to see him plunge entirely out of sight. Instead he sank just to the tops of his stovepipe boots. He unhooked his spectacles one-handed, wiped the lenses with the end of the blue bandanna around his neck, put them back on, and turned his dun parallel to the building at the foot of the slope. He rested his rifle across his saddle. He nestled his cheek against the stock, took in his breath, let part of it out, the vapor curling around his ears thick as spun sugar. His finger squeezed the trigger.

His horse showed no reaction to the crack of the report and the throb of the weapon lying across its back. Rawlings' untrained sorrel whistled and arched its spine, but he clamped his thighs tight, leaning back on the reins until the animal settled down; he was an experienced rider, if only in parks and on country lanes. When he was in a position to look at the weathervane, it was still spinning. A flock of crows startled from their perch in the pines wheeled against the sky, crying havoc.

Edwards leapt back aboard the dun. George squeaked out his Winchester. The Menéndezes' El Tigres were ready; they rested them across the throats of their saddles when they rode, alert for jackrabbits and prairie hens, tough and scrawny a meal as they made. Pierce, the close-up killer, drew his Navy Colt and checked the loads in the cylinder. Rawlings' rifle was a gas-fed Mauser from Pinkerton's arsenal, the newest weapon in the band; he held it by its pistol grip behind the square magazine. He'd spent a day with it on the range in San Francisco and had shown promise, if only for punching holes in paper targets. (He was less handy with the pocket pistol he'd been assigned; but the instructor said he wasn't likely to be called upon to shoot in close quarters: As it turned out, the man was wrong.)

They waited for a response from the building. They were

still waiting when the last of the crows returned to its branch and shrugged its feathers back into place.

St. John laid his Henry across his thighs. "Whose turn is it?"

"Whose is it always?" George kneed his mount forward and down the decline, leaning back for balance with his reins wrapped around one wrist. He held his carbine upright with his other hand, its buttstock braced on his thigh. The pinto read the terrain by feel, making lazy *S*'s and zigzags, its rider leaning now left, now right, like a man steering a boat without oars.

The ground leveled out twenty yards in front of the building. He stepped off and let the reins drop to the ground; the horse waggled its head but stayed put. The Indian appeared to hesitate, then returned the Winchester to its scabbard and drew his sidearm, a Starr revolver with a self-cocking hammer. He pulled back his shoulders (Rawlings could see the blades converging), found his way between the crowded firs to the porch, and climbed the steps, feeling each with a foot before trusting his weight to it. At the top he paused again, then reached out and tore open the door.

3

ROBBERS' ROOST

The sun, red as a railroad lantern, perched motionless on the line where earth met sky; even the mingled breath of the men and horses waiting on the ridge seemed painted in place. Rawlings gripped his saddle horn with his free hand, the Mauser's butt making a permanent dent in his thigh, waiting to hear the bark of gunfire from inside the building at the foot of the slope. Two minutes crawled past like a drop of sweat traveling down the back of his neck. Then George American Horse stepped out onto the deranged porch, holding his Winchester above his head. He shouted something, but the wind, abruptly remembering its function, snatched it away.

St. John clucked his tongue. His horse started down, accompanied by the others. George waited for them on the porch, holding his carbine now across his waist in both hands.

"Deserted," he said, when they drew up. "There's a corral out back just as empty."

The marshal raised his chin, sniffing the air. "Not so long you can't still smell it."

He dismounted, letting his reins fall, and climbed the porch, bootheels ringing on the frozen planks as on iron. George stepped aside to let him through the door. The rest of the party followed.

Rawlings was the only one who tied his horse to a post; it wasn't ground-trained. At the top he paused to stamp snow off his boots, feeling foolish for this mindless gesture to the hospitality of residents since departed—and criminals at that, if this fresh evidence supported St. John's hunch.

Paco and Diego didn't join them. So far as the Pinkerton could penetrate their mystery, they appeared to be more comfortable without a roof overhead.

Inside he waited for his eyes to adjust to the gloom. Like any empty building in snow country, this one was marrow-cold inside; his breath hung motionless in the space like cave mold. The walls and floor, both made of unplaned pine, were bare of anything but ample debris. Nothing in the room was true. A long cedarwood counter stood at a sharp angle along the back wall. The floor had collapsed beneath one end, lifting the other into a steep incline, as of a ship sinking. Crude shelves leaned out into the room, incompetent now of their purpose; piles of rusted tins, shattered bottles, and sprung rat-traps lay at their base. There was a primordial musk of moldy newspaper and rotting grain, leavened by the sickly sweet odor of fresh manure coming in from the back, where a door hung dementedly on hinges fashioned from harness leather. Another smell, more homey and almost welcome, issued from a fireplace hollowed out in the base of the stone chimney. Shingled ashes lay atop a dozen or so railroad spikes welded to make a grate.

St. John picked up a broken chair, shook his head, and let it drop; placed his hand against a wall, stroked it, shook his head again. He stepped to the fireplace, holding out his palms as if there were still warmth to be drawn from it.

"Is he doing what I think he is?" the Pinkerton whispered

to George, who was closest; and wondered why he whispered.

The Indian hissed at him to shut up.

"My mistake," said St. John then. "They didn't stay long enough to make themselves comfortable." He stooped, stirred a hand among the ashes, stacked like bricks, and fished out a scrap of paper scorched brown around all its edges. Standing, he turned it toward the fading light entering through the open front door, looked at it, holding it out at arm's length, then extended it to Edwards, who was standing closest to him. He wiped ash off on his trousers.

Edwards was still studying the fragment when Rawlings approached. He read the partial engraving over the sharpshooter's shoulder.

"Five hundred dollars! It's part of a bearer bond."

"The Buckners took eleven thousand in securities along with cash from that train at Elephant Crossing," St. John said. "I reckon it'd take at least that to make as much ash as this here."

"But it's the same as cash!"

"In San Francisco or New York, mebbe, where they might not look twice at it. Out here, you hand somebody a gold coin, he bites it to see is it lead. What do you think you'll get if you try to pass one of those, with wanted dodgers chasing you across two states?"

"A cot in a room with bars all around," Edwards said.

St. John shook his head yet again; he looked almost pleased. "It's no wonder I couldn't get a line on this crew. I been ordering from Sears and Roebuck when I should've been shopping uptown."

"As picturesque as that sounds, Marshal, I've no idea what it means."

"I do." Edwards dropped the scrap and crushed it with a toe. "Anyone who'd throw back a fish this size is out to hook something bigger." He looked at St. John. "How'd you know this was the place to leave the train behind?"

It was George who answered. "Don't you know? He's got a gift." Rawlings could never tell when the man was mocking or dead serious.

St. John lifted a shoulder, let it drop. "It's halfway between Elephant Crossing and Pinto Creek; and it's the kind of place I'd pick."

He started toward the back door. Rawlings fell in behind, trailed closely by the others.

The corral had been built behind the building, of pine boughs stripped of their greenery and supported by stout posts fashioned from trunks. The wood was yellow; it had worn bark until recently. The wind had picked up, blowing dry snow into clouds like smoke from a brushfire. The earth beneath had been torn and trampled by hooves. Yellow grain littered the ground in sodden heaps.

"Looks like the Pinkertons are good for something besides breaking up strikes and questioning my judgment," St. John said. "We found where the Buckners hid some of their pirate gold; the four-legged kind. They stopped here just long enough to pasture their spent mounts and throw their saddles on the fresh."

Rawlings said, "George was right. We might be able to overtake them this side of Wyoming."

"Probably not them; but *some*one's been here to pick up the horses they played out and drive 'em, I'm guessing, to Pinto Creek. Him we might catch."

"Him who?"

"What George overheard back at the zinc mine? I'm thinking the Carol they were fixing to meet up with isn't a woman after all. I could be wrong, but wrangling horses is generally man's work."

4

PINTO CREEK

George and Edwards dismantled enough of the corral to build a fire in the base of the chimney, using dried horse chips for kindling. The seven men spread their bedrolls on the floor and sat, backs resting against their saddles, carefully sipping the boiling coffee, bandannas wrapped around the tin cups to protect their hands. The Menéndezes raised their stock in the company by roasting and passing around portions of small game they'd shot on sticks over the fire, then sat apart to eat theirs in relative silence. The food was tough and stringy; but after long monotonous hours aboard train followed by a trek through belly-deep snow on horseback, it was as good as anything served in a restaurant in San Francisco. Afterwards St. John lit a Simón Bolívar and held the burning branch from the fire to ignite George's cheroot and the cigarettes the Mexicans smoked, rolled in twists of brown paper; they contained an Indian blend of some kind that smelled like burning brush.

In the cherry glow from the hearth, Edwards produced a rectangular brown bottle from a deep pocket of his corduroy coat and thumbed out the cork. It was smaller than a deck of cards. He offered it around.

St. John took it and shook the contents. "How long you been keeping this secret?"

"Just since the mine. I been saving it for when this here

enterprise turns out to be more than just a snipe hunt. I traded a prospector a plug of tobacco for it."

"You barely got back your bait." St. John swigged, bunched his face into creases. "He saw you coming, Bill. Somebody brewed this from a core sample." He passed it to George, who took a shallower draft, then gave it to Rawlings, who sampled it to be sociable; he wasn't abstemious, but he preferred to drink in more civilized circumstances. The whiskey scorched his throat, but then a euphoric heat spread out from the floor of his stomach, forcing the chill from all his extremities; even the tips of his ears burned. He returned the bottle to Edwards, who reached out to offer it to the Menéndezes. Surprisingly, they made no move to accept it.

"Holding out for champagne, I guess." He drank and started it around again.

"It's Sunday," said Pierce, who'd refused as well. "Even papists respect the Sabbath."

George had been silent; now he spoke.

"Ike, you know damn well the cavalry translated my father's name to American Horse from the Absaroka. I took it up when I left Fort Lincoln, and I was going by it when you killed Drebber. No one called me George till they enrolled me in mission school later, and I sure as hell wasn't named after your damn chestnut."

By this time, the marshal's face was mostly in darkness, the firelight illuminating it only as far as his moustaches; the shadow of his hatbrim obscured the rest. When he drew on the cigar, his eyes glittered in the glow.

"Sure, George, if that's how you remember it." He poured half a jigger's worth from the bottle into his cup. "You know, it's funny how coffee never tastes as good after the first sip. It needs a boost every other time."

Edwards laughed. George shook his head and held out his cup for more whiskey. Rawlings wondered just how many hours he'd wasted transcribing the marshal's memoirs into his notebooks. They might have been cribbed from Paul Bunyan and Pecos Bill.

The subject needed changing. He asked what the plan was for Pinto Creek.

St. John rolled his shoulders. "We'll ask around. It's a small town; everybody knows everybody, and strangers stick out like tits on a snake."

"Including us. The natives out here don't feel the same obligation to citizenship that they do back East."

"We'll place our faith in western hospitality."

"I don't know what that means."

"The ungracious shall seek mercy, and be denied."

St. John looked at Pierce, sitting with his Bible tilted toward the firelight. "The Word of the Lord?"

"Of His humble servant."

"What all that means is us folks on the border got the reputation for accommodating strangers on account of we'll get shot if we don't." Edwards took his turn with the bottle.

Rawlings said, "You can't always trust what you get at gunpoint. There'd be no need for lawmen if you could."

"Well, let's all sleep on that." The marshal flipped the dregs of his cup into the fire and sent the stub of his cigar after it. "Mebbe I'll tag on to the end of whatever Race Buckner dreamt about when he was here."

A half-day north of Mercury City, the Indian raised his chin, sniffed at the air, and guided his pinto at a walk some fifty yards off the path, where he dismounted and pawed at a depression in the snow with a foot. He uncovered a patch of black ash and charred stubs of pine; the wind carried an acrid odor to the others watching from the trail. Lowering himself on one knee, he felt the embers, then stepped back into leather and rejoined the party.

"Two days or a year," he reported. "Take your pick."

"George, I don't know what we'd do without you." St. John gathered his reins.

"That's just what you said when I came to Fort Smith looking for work with the Indian police."

"Recognized you right off. You'd growed more out than up."

Just before nightfall they found evidence more heartening. On a bald hill scraped almost bare by wind, a trail of irregular green-brown spheres like unjacketed walnuts brought George out of the saddle again, to pick one up, crumble it between his palms, and stoop to cleanse his hands in snow. "You don't often see this many prairie oysters outside a parade; and they're not froze clear through. We didn't miss friend Carol more than a day at the corral."

They camped twice, but no more whiskey made its appearance and they ate venison jerky they'd traded for in Elephant Crossing, soaking it in water from their canteens to spare their teeth; coffee was out, as St. John had decided against keeping a fire.

"Figure we're as close as that?" Edwards said.

"You won't find a better judge of horseshit than George. We might keep him around a mite longer after all."

The Crow chewed on his unlit cheroot and said something guttural. Pierce muttered something in response that Rawlings didn't expect to find in the Sermon on the Mount.

* * *

Observed from the top of a rise, Pinto Creek, Wyoming, was a clump of matter that might have settled in the bottom of a dry wash; an accident of nature rather than a city plan. On closer observation, it might have been any town out West. Two rows of frame buildings with false second stories faced each other across a street broad enough to turn around a wagon—not that it seemed there was anything in the place worth going back for. Every structure seemed to serve a double purpose: General merchandise/town hall, livery/blacksmith's, bank/post office, schoolhouse/church, saloon/bawdyhouse; Rawlings wondered if some deluded founding father had wanted to leave room for a modern metropolis.

The newcomers had pushed hard since before dawn in order to reach the town before noon. The horses were lathered, and layers of sweat sheathed the riders beneath their coats in spite of the cold. They stepped down in front of the livery/blacksmith's, staggering into the pool of their shadows. St. John ordered the others to separate into parties of two, asking after strangers, particularly any with horses for sale. "That'll be our man's cut of the take," he said. "I don't expect he'll be spending it in the collection plate at church; but don't overlook it. If such as Testament can see the light, there's hope for a thief."

Pierce set his jaw, but said nothing. Rawlings didn't know if he objected to St. John's remark or the nickname he'd given him.

The marshal did the pairing: Edwards got the Mexicans; St. John, Rawlings. St. John looked at George and Pierce. "You two play nice."

"'Love thine enemy,'" Edwards told the Indian.

"Go to hell."

The door to the livery was padlocked. The blacksmith on the other side of the wall separating the establishments, shirtless under his overalls with biceps like knotted rope, knew nothing about strangers or strange horses. He said the livery manager had gone home to eat, but would be back sometime that afternoon. St. John and Rawlings crossed to the barbershop, in a stone building with a striped pole on one side of the door and a chipped sign on the other reading JAIL. Rawlings commented on that.

"Not so loco as you might think," said St. John. "Ninety days between haircuts sounds about right."

They went inside. Here there was no partition. One side of the room contained a hydraulic chair, a three-by-six-foot mirror, an oak washstand and cabinets, a small writing table, and a set of personalized shaving mugs on a rack; the other a cot, separated from the rest of the room by iron strips riveted together to form a lattice. Someone lay snoring on the cot with his back to the room. The only inhabitant on their side of the cage stood before the mirror with his galluses down and no collar, carefully scraping lather from around his black muttonchops with a cutthroat razor. He was built slight and had a bald spot the shape of a bootheel on the back of his head; it was as if he'd been kicked by a mule and the hair had never grown back. Spotting the visitors in reflection, he winked, breaking that side of his face into a mass of wrinkles. *A born winker,* Rawlings thought.

"You the barber or the sheriff?" St. John said.

The man flicked lather into the basin in front of him and wiped the blade on a striped towel hanging from a rung mounted under the mirror. "That depends on whether you're looking for a shave or a place to make a complaint. From the looks of you it could be either one." He mopped soap off his face, hung up the towel, and turned their way, drawing as he did so a Sharps pistol from a socket next to the rung. A nickel-plated star on his shirt winked in the light, as if to mock the man it was pinned to. "Burt Fabian, sheriff—till the end of the year, anyway. The voters of Logan County studied the matter and decided it was time for a change; but that's all right. Folks will always need barbers."

St. John held his hands away from his body. "Slow day, I'm guessing, to have to force a man into your chair at gun-point."

"Just at the moment I'm serving the city." Fabian gestured with the revolver. "You first; left hand. You ain't wearing no cross-draw."

St. John nudged Rawlings, who understood, raising both hands. When the marshal let his gun belt slip to his feet with a clunk, the sheriff gestured Rawlings' way. "Take your time, son; like they're your last minutes on earth."

Rawlings lowered his hands to inch the Thunderer from his coat pocket, holding the butt between his thumb and index finger, and bent his knees in order to ease it to the floor. Straightening, he said, "This man is a peace officer. I'm a Pinkerton operative. I have papers."

"You're no lefty neither. Use that one. I been fooled by hideouts before."

They were in his left-hand pocket. He drew out the oilskin wrap, opened it slowly, and held up the documents, including the order signed by the governor of Wyoming. Fabian took them and looked them over at an angle that kept them in the tail of his eye. He returned the papers and looked at St. John. When he smiled his entire face collapsed in wrinkles; it was as if there were no bones to give it structure. "I seen right off we had a thing in common. I got a brother-in-law in Joplin voted for you!"

"I been wondering who that was. We ain't here to make a complaint. We sure enough could use a shave, but that'll keep." The marshal retrieved his gun belt and buckled it on. Rawlings picked up his Colt and pocketed it along with the papers in their pouch.

"Now that we're all friends," St. John said.

Fabian turned and slid the pistol back into its socket. "I ain't always this nervous. Man in that cell's got friends of his own."

The visitors turned for another look at the man on the cot. The marshal said, "I'll climb out on a limb and say he goes by Carol."

5

THE MAN ON THE COT

The shaving mugs on the wall rack rattled, then jingled, china against china. From the street out front came a hoarse chortling noise, a series of pops, as by someone discharging light loads from a pistol, then a single ear-splitting report, and finally a wheeze, like air escaping a ruptured bellows. Rawlings plunged a hand into the pocket containing his revolver; St. John's Colt was already in his fist.

Burt Fabian shook his head and pulled his galluses up over his narrow shoulders. "That's just Grady Stern and that gas-powered go-devil his wife left him over. Try not to shoot him. He can't afford the burial."

On the other side of the plate-glass window, an appliance of red enamel mounted on black rubber took up most of the hitching rail in front of the barbershop, partially obscured by a final gasp of smoke drifting forward from its posterior. It had twin brass carriage lamps up front, more painted metal behind (brown rather than red, under a skin of road grit), and behind that a fat man wearing a linen duster and a visored cap, grappling with a lever that didn't seem to want to go where it was intended. Finally—having either won the contest or given it up as hopeless—he climbed down from his high seat and hopped onto the boardwalk that ran past the shop, stripping off a pair of leather gauntlets as he approached the door. A copper bell tinkled when he opened it.

"Burt, what can you do with this here mop?" He snatched off his cap, exposing a thatch of straw-colored hair tangled like brass-wire.

"Not just now, Grady. I'm busy keeping the peace and protecting the sonsabitches that run me out of office."

The man took in the two trailworn strangers still holding firearms. His face went the color of white lead.

"Not them." Fabian tipped his head toward the man still asleep in the cell. "Him."

He looked. "The drunk? I heard about that; but—"

"Oh, he owes Lars Nordlund for damages to the fixtures down at the Babylon. These fellows are just here to guard the thirty-two-fifty till I get it under lock and key. You can't be too careful with them Buckners about."

"Oh. Sure can't. Well, I got spark plugs on order at Milliken's. I'll be back."

"Hang onto some change. You owe me for the last two times." When Grady drew the door shut behind him, Fabian looked at the others. "He ain't made the acquaintance of two nickels the same day since he bought that pile of pig iron."

"He's right about one thing," said St. John. "All this seems like a deal of trouble to go to over some busted glass."

"Well, there's the hole in the back wall looking into Countess Franzini's place of business. Also this here." The sheriff opened a drawer in the oak washstand and took out a limp fold of leather that looked as if it had been fished from a pond and left out in the sun to dry and forgotten about. He spread it open gingerly and extracted a square of yellowed paper in similar condition. As carefully as he unfolded it, it fell into four pieces disintegrating at the edges. He offered it cupped in both hands to the marshal, who accepted it the same way. Once-bold lettering had receded into pulp, formerly coarse and now rubbed soft as fine linen:

REWARD

$500 (FIVE HUNDRED DOLLARS)

for the arrest and conviction of

Llewellyn Carroll Underwood

Alias L.C. Wood, Carroll Wood, Lew Woodrow, and etc.

WANTED

for the train robbery at Blue Cut, Missouri, September 7, 1881

Under the amount of the reward was a pen-and-ink sketch of a dark-bearded man with a hairline that ran straight across his brow less than two inches above the eyes. The face itself had faded almost to a blank oval. The picture might have been drawn by a child with a fair sense of proportion, and bore a vague enough resemblance to the general population to support the arrest of any American male of a certain age for questioning.

St. John said as much to the sheriff, who nodded, absently massaging the back of his head as if to encourage hair on the bald patch.

"Twenny-five years don't change that. If I'd knowed he was such a customer I'd of went with Milt Jackson when Nordlund sent his boy with the news from the saloon. Now I got a deputy at home with three busted ribs and an ear bit off. They'd still be rolling around there in the sawdust fixing to gouge out each other's eyes if I didn't go over to see what was taking so long and buffaloed the old bastard from ambush with Penelope there." He pointed at the socketed gun. "He's got him a head like a scalding pot."

"That all you're holding him on?"

"It was enough till I found out he tried selling four played-out horses to Oscar Bundt at the livery. Oscar smelt a rat and throwed him out. He's been skinned before, so he says."

Rawlings asked if he'd had a bill of sale.

"That's what stuck in Oscar's nose. It was dated down in Pueblo just last week. J.P. Morgan didn't make his first million buying horses and selling 'em two weeks later for the same money when all they need is a good rubdown and a couple days' rest. I figured to hold him till I got word on my wire to Pueblo, but after I seen that there paper it occurred to me he might have friends to go with them horses and they might come to see what's keeping him." He watched St. John stack the tattered pieces of bulletin and place them in his own wallet, as delicately as if he were pressing a flower between the pages of a book. "That bounty's no good now, or I'd of claimed it myself. The governor that posted it's six feet closer to hell."

"I'm starting a museum. What else did he have on him?"

A gold tooth caught the light in a grin. The sheriff opened one of the oak cabinets, pulled out a woven basket with a handle, and rested it on the washstand.

The visitors peered down at the collection inside: A big-bore Remington revolver in a greasy chamois-leather holster, a pair of pepperbox pistols, a two-shot .22 derringer with its front sight filed off, and a Bowie knife with a cedar handle worn smooth from handling and a steel knob on the end.

"Sealed the deal for me," said Fabian. "If every man with Custer was heeled like that, he'd be president now. I told the old cob he's lucky I come along before he fell in the Platte and sunk to the bottom."

St. John lifted out the Bowie and slid off its cowhide sheath, revealing a blade wide enough for a machete. He tested the edge with the ball of his thumb, releasing a spring of blood. He sucked the thumb, resheathed the blade, and spun the knife, the handle toward Rawlings. "Here. Souvenir for you."

"'Your young men have I slain with the sword.'"

Something in Midian Pierce's voice, syrupy yet bitter, like thistle honey, moved the Pinkerton to accept the knife without hesitation. The Sunday school teacher had entered in company with George American Horse and Wild Bill Edwards, somehow without disturbing the bell on the door.

George said, "Livery just opened up. It's boarding four horses that make everything else in the stable look like ground squirrels; but I'm guessing you know that already." He'd taken in the scene.

A flatulent squawk drew all eyes to the window, where the Mexicans were loitering around Grady Stern's automobile. One of them had squeezed the rubber bulb belonging to the horn perched on a fender. From this perspective the contraption looked like a Chinese lacquered tea cart with industrial features added on; the questionable tastes of two centuries combined in one package.

"My men," St. John told Fabian, who'd turned to retrieve his pistol. To the others: "We could've took our time. The sheriff had the situation in hand." He tilted his head toward the cell.

Just then Rawlings heard the hollow cluck-cluck of a pendulum and noticed the cuckoo clock on the wall for the first time. The man on the cot had quit snoring. The Pinkerton locked gazes with a pair of eyes glittering in the half-light of the cell; he'd been stared at just like that by an old lion in a cage in San Francisco, with the same yellow eyes. The prisoner had rolled over to face the group without making a sound.

"We'll take him off your hands," St. John said, "seeing as he's awake."

"You'll settle his bill first."

St. John stretched a hand toward Rawlings. "Deal me one of them John Does."

The unwieldy knife was now a preposterous impediment, like an umbrella on a sunny day. He reached behind him, lifting his coattails and tucking it under his belt, brought out the oilskin, and withdrew a blank arrest warrant from the sheaf the Agency had provided, signed by a federal judge. "It has to be filled in."

"Make it out to our new traveling companion."

"Which name should I use?"

"Box the compass."

Rawlings borrowed the writing table (the Bowie's handle burrowing a hole in his spine), dipped its pen in the ink well, wrote *L.C. Underwood* in the blank, and gave the paper to the marshal, who handed it to Fabian without looking at it. The sheriff studied it as if it were an unidentified species of foliage.

St. John said, "Give the saloonkeeper the rest of the iron you got off him. Hell, sell it along with the horses and split the money; you'll both be to the good. Don't tell me you didn't already think of that. Just leave us one to carry our prisoner. Hang on." He plucked one of the pepperbox pistols from the basket and slid it into a coat pocket. "There's no telling when I might have to shoot myself out of a room full of Republicans."

6

THE LAST BUSHWHACKER

"I can bring in the Mexicans," St. John said. "That is, if you think eight guns is enough."

The hoop Burt Fabian had taken down off its nail contained only one key, but it didn't look lonely; it was bronze, weighed at least half a pound, and in a pinch would do for a bludgeon. He'd switched it to his left hand in order to take the big revolver in his right. He waggled it.

"Laugh all you want. I had to thump him three times yesterday before he knew I was there."

Wild Bill Edwards had gone to the livery to fetch one of the horses Underwood had brought to town, along with his riding gear. George American Horse was sent out to the marshal's claybank to bring back a pair of manacles from the saddlebags.

The old man stumbled off his cot and out into the relative freedom of the barbershop, leaning his weight on the bars while he shook circulation back into one leg. Blood crusted his bald crown and matted his dishwater beard; this for some reason he'd tied into a queue with cord, along with what was left of his hair, drawing the skin of his face tight to the skull: Sores ran on his cheeks and caruncular nose where the bones had worried through the flesh. His shirt was sun-bleached calico, the sleeves curiously gussetted and buttoned snug to his wrists; Rawlings thought of pictures of pirates he'd seen in books. The garment hung on him like bunting. His trousers were filthy, blown out at the knees, his boots worn flannel-thin at the toes; heels and soles had merged. The past had embossed itself on every inch of his five-and-a-half feet.

The Indian came with the handcuffs; D-shaped clamps of dull gunmetal steel connected by three links of chain.

"Treat him gentle, George."

He looked at St. John. "On account of he's old?"

"On account of he belongs in a glass case like the king's jewels, and not out in the open where any whelp fresh off the tit can set a match to his whiskers just because they're white. Blue Cut was Frank and Jesse's last job in Missouri. That's a genuine guerrilla shirt he's wearing, bought with Union plunder. They don't make 'em since Sherman burnt all the cotton fields in Dixie. You're looking at the only surviving member of the James-Younger Gang: the West's last bushwhacker."

Rawlings blew a gust of unamused laughter. "A thief's a thief, no matter who he rode with and what he wears on his back."

"Mebbe so. But I don't feature to slap him around so bad he drops dead and I wind up keeping company in the history books with that back-shooting maggot Bob Ford."

"You have a distorted idea of history, Marshal."

St. John watched George clamp on the irons. Underwood showed no resistance, apart from that yellow glare. He hadn't opened his mouth once. It seemed to have healed shut like an old wound.

"You ain't been around long enough to know what's history and what isn't," said St. John, "pup like you. Look at Paco and Diego out there: They say they're freedom fighters, but I got a twenty-dollar gold piece says the only thing they ever freed was a hundred pesos' worth of silver from the pantry of some Spanish grandee south of the border, with help from the houseboy. But they're here, that's the difference. It's the survivors that tell the story."

The Menéndezes turned that way from the street, as if they'd overheard him through the thick plate glass. Grady Stern was there too, scowling at the pair. They hadn't lost their fascination with his automobile; but apart from shifting his sack of merchandise from one arm to the other, he made no move. Those Mexican repeaters seemed to have grown to their hands.

Edwards had come in from tying up the extra horse. "Shame on you, George. You ought to have brung your best beads and feathers for the occasion."

"Heathen pomp," muttered Pierce.

"Let's ride," St. John said. "A little sun and fresh air might just pry him open. Sure enough he's got yarns worth listening to."

"Be a change. If I was to hear that Jack LeFever story one more time I might just turn outlaw myself." Edwards was grinning.

St. John's face went flat.

"We can't have that, Bill. The shock just might stop your heart."

They went outside, George and Wild Bill supporting the old man by his elbows, guns in their off hands, St. John and Rawlings covering him from behind and Pierce bringing up the rear. Paco and Diego, alerted by the activity, stood spread apart in the street gripping their Winchesters. Sheriff Fabian glowered from the doorway. He appeared uncertain about whether he'd come out ahead or behind on the deal. "Go home, Grady. I ain't selling haircuts today."

The motorist stepped from the path of the procession and

up onto the vehicle's running board. He turned a switch on the curved panel facing the driver's seat, picked up a crank from the floor on the passenger's side, and went around to the front to insert it. Edwards, holstering his gun, surrendered his place at the prisoner's side to Pierce and stepped around the motorcar to untie the sleek sorrel he'd selected from the stable. It looked fresh and ready to ride once again.

Stern wound the crank twice, drawing a spark, a sputter, and then a combustive burst from the motor. A ball of black smoke exploded from the tailpipe with a report that shook the glass in the barbershop window. The sorrel screamed and reared. The sharpshooter grabbed the reins in both hands. All heads swung that way but one.

Underwood pivoted on his left foot, swinging his manacled fists sideways and up, just grazing Pierce's jaw but hitting the muscle on the side of his neck full on. The Sunday school teacher stumbled. The prisoner followed through with his whole body, dumping him off the edge of the boardwalk and knocking George out of balance in the process. Pierce fell onto his back in the street. His hat landed on the edge of its flat brim and rolled.

"Testament, no!" But St. John's shout was lost in the roar of the motor and clatter of pistons.

Pierce sprang to his feet, his hair in his eyes, the Navy Colt leveling itself as he came up. The blast, too, was lost; orange-and-blue flame from the muzzle propelled a ball across the front of the jittering automobile and square between the shoulderblades of the last bushwhacker in the West.

7

PICTURE DAY

Their packhorse was ugly, a shaggy, awkward combination of all the things an experienced trader looked for when he needed an excuse to select another animal. Buck-kneed, slack-bellied, spavined, chronically fistulous, and with a neck seemingly incapable of supporting its overlarge head—and that in a constant fog—it would lack depth, stamina, and plain horse sense. Rawlings knew horses; this was barely of the species.

However, Irons St. John had pronounced it sound back in St. Louis, offering no explanation (itself an allusion to his mastery of the mystic arts); and much to the Pinkerton's annoyance, the beast had proven itself over five hundred miles of rough country, with only the occasional application of a chewing-tobacco poultice to heal its cankers. The situation grated every time Rawlings was obliged to retrieve something from a pack. It would almost be worth the hardship to find the creature lying belly to the sky, its stretched tether lifting its head, eyes turned up like rollers in a slot machine and the long yellow fingers of its teeth exposed in a ghastly mocking grin.

These thoughts stirred in the back of his brain as he lifted a flap and withdrew the square box of his Kodak in its rubber pouch.

It was roughly the size of a collar box, with a brass key on top, a sort of peephole on one end and a circular glass lens opposite it: the very first model of portable camera available, and it was Agency property. The entire device with its one hundred exposures had to be sent to the Eastman laboratories in upstate New York for opening under the proper conditions for processing.

The motorcar was gone, along with its operator, when he returned to the barbershop. Two separate crowds had gathered on either end of the boardwalk, held in check by the Mexicans with their carbines cradled in the crooks of their arms. Some of the gawkers wore shop aprons, and there were two or three women dressed for town in printed bonnets, their hands stuck in fur muffs. A little girl in ribbons straddled the neck of a farmer in overalls, craning for a better look.

The door to the shop was off its hinges, tipped against the front of the building, with George and Edwards standing on either side, set to catch the dead man between them if he started to slide. He was posed with his head tilted back against the door and his arms bent, as if prepared to reach for either the heavy revolver on the gun belt someone had buckled around his waist or the pepperbox pistol with its bundle of barrels stuck under the belt on the other side. For all that, he looked less martial than he had with only his eyes for weapons; they were still open, but the fire there no longer smoldered. He was just a bald old man in whiskers and rags with a dot of dried blood in one corner of his mouth like tobacco spittle, dead as Pharaoh.

A pane of glass behind his head read PRINCE OF WALES TONSORIAL PARLOUR in neat white letters.

Rawlings said, "I said I need his boots off."

"Just take the picture."

He looked at St. John leaning in the empty doorway. Behind him, Midian Pierce sat in Fabian's adjustable chair, his Bible spread before him still bristling with scraps of paper stuck between pages: mile markers along the journey to Enlightenment.

"They must be off or the measurements won't be accurate. Chicago requires them for identification."

"Then don't take it."

"He's dead. What does it matter if he has holes in his socks?"

"Nothing don't matter no more." This was Fabian, sitting on the edge of the boardwalk with his feet in the street, nursing a flat green bottle he'd produced from somewhere. "I counted on making up for my sheriff's salary once the developers bought the right-of-way off the railroad outside town. All them pilgrims will need to have their hair cut to look good in church. This here's the first shooting we had in ten years. Cheyenne lost out on the same deal when they hung Tom Horn there." He was ignored.

"I didn't see anything about your soft spot for criminals in *The Iron Star*," Rawlings told St. John.

"I was one once, don't forget. J. Mercer Fleet didn't say anything about that neither." He straightened away from the doorway and held out a hand. "I'm borrowing back that Bowie."

The Pinkerton was thrown off his subject. "What for?"

"Pretty him up. Chicago can publish it in the *Tribune*, play it up as Jesse's last ride; be so tickled they won't notice what he's got on his feet."

Dazed by this exercise in logic, Rawlings drew the knife from under his coattails, stepped up on the boardwalk, and laid it on the marshal's palm. Framed in the viewfinder with the immense blade stuck under his belt, the dead man recovered some of the aspect of that lion in a cage. Rawlings snapped the shutter, advanced the film, and struck another shot for security. He wound the key again to the next frame, then dropped the camera into its pouch and drew the string tight. "I forgot you were a politician."

"So did most of the voters in Missouri. Lay him flat, George. He's starting to look like an advertisement."

With Edwards' help, George lowered the door to the boardwalk. One of Underwood's arms flopped over the side. Rigor mortis—or more likely rheumatism—had cramped his fingers into a fist.

Pierce joined the group, the Bible making a bulge in his side pocket.

St. John looked at Fabian. "This town have an undertaker?"

Edwards said, "Sure it does. Probably shares the place with a taxidermist."

"Down the alley," Fabian said. "I guess he'll give you the county rate. Fifteen dollars."

"If that's the county rate, let the county pay for it. It happened in your jail."

"They'll stick me with it if I try. I'm a busted flush since election day. Anyway, I surrendered custody." He leaned over and patted the vest pocket with the warrant folded up inside. He almost dropped his bottle.

St. John ran a hand over the stubble on his chin. "Got any more of that tanglefoot? Killing's thirsty work."

Muttering, Fabian gathered up his limbs and went inside, clearing the doorframe on the second try. When he was out of sight, the marshal turned to the Sunday school teacher. "I told you not to shoot."

The smooth face was bland. "I couldn't hear you over the noise of that infernal machine."

"You're deaf when it suits you."

Rawlings wanted to remind him that Pierce's ready finger on the trigger was supposed to be his contribution to the enterprise, but thought better of it.

The sheriff returned, carrying a soda-pop crate loaded with more flat green bottles. "Medicine show I run out of town left 'em behind. Says on the label you're guaranteed against ring-worm for life."

"'Left 'em behind.'" Edwards grinned. "Absent-minded, them tambourine-thumpers." He stooped, snatched out a bottle, and held it up against the sun. Tiny flat particles eddied inside like minnows in a brook.

"Well, pass 'em around, Bill," St. John said. "An ounce of prevention's worth a pound of cure."

Edwards did so. Rawlings took a sip. The liquor was laced with honey or molasses and tried to climb back up his throat.

"What's the difference where we put him?" George nudged the recumbent door with his toe. "We can chuck him in the creek. It isn't a glass case, but it's better than anything the James boys handed out."

St. John said, "We'll dig a hole someplace."

Edwards swallowed, dragged a sleeve across his lips. "I didn't sign on to do spade work."

"We'll dig a hole, put up a cross, and Testament will read over him. You can take off your hat, if that ain't too much like honest labor."

Wild Bill appeared to have worn out his welcome with the marshal, Rawlings observed; Pierce's rebuke had been mild in comparison. How many more men must the pious killer shoot in the back to earn the same disfavor? Truly this was foreign country.

8

WYOMING PASTORALE

Irons St. John's gaze lit on the now-superfluous horse tied up at the rail, wearing the dead man's saddle, a sorry piece of leather with bits of bark and sawdust clinging to it. He pointed the neck of his bottle that direction.

"Swap that to the undertaker for his work," he told the sheriff, "or sell it and settle up with him. It ought to bring in enough for a decent coffin and a chunk of marble and maybe a psalm or two. If you keep the horse and chuck that old sinner in a crick I'll find out. Meantime you better learn to swim."

Fabian's face was flushed, and only partly from drink. "What about my door? Snow's coming."

George and Edwards were directed to the task of setting the door back up on its hinges. They took the corpse under the arms and by the legs and lifted it over onto the boardwalk.

St. John frowned at the dead man lying on the bare planks. He caught the sheriff's eye. "He didn't come here in his shirt-sleeves."

"Just a ratty old buffalo coat. It's out back covering fire-wood."

"Get it."

When he returned, carrying a shaggy bundle with bald patches, the marshal took it and spread it over the dead man.

By then the crowd had drifted away. Rawlings shielded his eyes against the sun. "We have only four hours left of daylight."

"That'll take us halfway to Cheyenne. The Buckners are sure to put in there for supplies and provisions; maybe some lewd women, if we're lucky and they don't know we're stepping on their heels. We'll camp on the trail." He turned and stuck out a hand. "Obliged for your help, Sheriff."

Rawlings watched them shake hands. St. John had as many sides as a diamond, but it was rare to see them all in the course of a single day.

Whatever his faults as a peace officer—Rawlings had no point of reference to judge his barbering skills—Burt Fabian knew a thing or two about the weather. Just before dusk the wind picked up off the Rockies, blowing a squall of powdered-glass flakes that blinded them as they sought the shelter of a ridge where they could set up camp.

As ridges go, it was considerable. If Colorado was all boulders and hardpack, Wyoming was a great extinct beast, too huge and proud to have died anywhere but out in the open. Its spine showed in a dorsal curve of granite, polished white by countless millennia of wind, drought, and snow. George unwrapped the slicker from his bedroll and held it up as a windbreak while the rest coaxed a fire from twigs and leaves, plundering their store of matches on damp branches of local pine and blowing on the sparks until they caught. In this the Mexicans displayed patience none of their companions expected of them, apart from St. John: "Give them Yaquis two sticks to scrape together and they'll get a rock to burn in a monsoon."

The snow stopped around midnight, the wind shortly thereafter; Rawlings, swaddled in his bedroll, read the time on his internal clock; he had his months with the Cattleman's Trust in Denver to thank for that. He hadn't slept. At length he rose, gathered his blanket around him, and walked creaking through a snowfall that seemed to come with its own source of light, guided by the single orange eye of a burning cigar to where St. John sat half-reclined against his saddle. There was no reason now to fret about smoke, either from one of his Bolívars or the campfire. By now the Buckners would be burrowed in Cheyenne, no question; the lawman expected all his quarry to proceed as if he'd directed their movements personally. *Like Napoleon at Austerlitz,* Rawlings thought.

Around them was the sound of even, measured breathing, punctuated at odd intervals by snorts and the occasional flatulent bleat. The two men might have been the only creatures awake for miles.

"Can't sleep, or won't?" St. John greeted.

Rawlings sat beside him, cross-legged in his blanket, like Indians he'd seen at railroad stations. (They were fixtures in every public place, peddling clay pots and beaded belts. One, an Arapaho, had traded him information for the price of a drink of rum and his trunk key, which the man admired for a trinket. The information proved useless, as St. John predicted. Rawlings couldn't imagine he'd never seen an Indian before George.) It was too cold for the snow to melt from the heat of his body; in fact, it provided warmth, as every sled dog that curled up in it in the north country was aware.

"Both. I don't sleep well in the best of circumstances."

"Me either. Lost the habit in Alaska. Up there they measure day and night by the calendar. I had trouble in broad daylight, and then when it was over I couldn't get used to the dark; and what's worse, when I got back, I couldn't get used to how it was before I left." He blew a dense cloud that cast a silver shadow on the snow.

"I didn't know you were in Alaska." That was troubling: The Pinkerton had considered himself an expert on the man's past, based on his research. Was the Agency's records system not omniscient after all?

St. John seemed to have read his thoughts. "No reason you should. You won't see it in Fleet's book. I went up there with a wagonload of canvas, looking to get rich selling tent material to prospectors, but I come too late. Them that had made their stake had built cabins, and them that hadn't had shipped back to Seattle and Frisco with their tails between their legs. I tried my hand with a pick and shovel, but the rush was over. I left most of my truck behind and got into politics. I reckon you'd say I have a talent for dropping my line in a rain barrel hoping for catfish." When he drew in smoke, the tip glowed fiercely, illuminating fresh creases on his face.

The other shook his head. "I've given up trying to tell when you're stretching the account."

"Me also, where you're concerned. I can't decide whether the Pinkertons recruit born liars or provide special training."

Rawlings wasn't surprised; which surprised him. He supposed he'd known all along his fraud was transparent. Here was an invitation to clear the air, and he was either too tired or too disillusioned to bother turning it down.

"This is as close as I've ever been to Cheyenne. When I finished training in San Francisco they put me behind a desk. I always thought I'd be reassigned to the field, but I'm too good with numbers and organization. Almost everything I've told you about my experience was handed to me in a file. I'm a fair shot, but that's never been tested except on the range. I've never killed a man, in Mexico or anyplace else. I'm telling you this because it will all be clear when we get to Cheyenne."

"Well, you didn't miss much there; and when it comes to killing, everybody's a natural."

"Rot. I'm not Pierce. He could put down his Bible in the middle of a passage, commit murder, then pick it back up and go on from where he left off. He was born to it. George and Wild Bill are the same, except in their case it comes from practice. I'm likely to freeze when the time comes and get us all killed."

St. John was silent for a while. In the stillness of a winter night in the immense dome that was Wyoming, the hiss of his burning cigar and the soft pop when he puffed at it were as loud as an axe splitting wood.

"Getting killed is easier still," he said. "And you only have to do it once."

"I'm sure you think that's a comfort."

"I'm thinking leave the thinking to the enemy." He took the cigar from his mouth, looked at the end, and flicked it away. It described a bright orange parabola against black sky and sank into the snow out of sight with a sizzle. "It's Pierce's secret; leastwise the only one that concerns us. That's advice, which I'm guessing is what you come for."

"I came to clear the air."

"Next time don't. I got cares enough to keep me up nights without taking on yours too." St. John pulled up his covers and rolled himself into them, turning his back on the Pinkerton. "Try to sleep. There's going to be killing tomorrow, or I've lost my edge. You want to be awake for that."

9

CHEYENNE

"Will you look at this place?" St. John said. "I used to be able to find my way to every whorehouse in town in the dark, but now I wouldn't know where to start. It's like they took Philadelphia apart and put it back together here in buffalo country."

They'd stopped their horses to take in Cheyenne from the west end of a principal street built almost entirely of brick on both sides, with advertisements for Coca-Cola and Singer Sewing Machines painted on the walls facing alleys; such frame buildings as remained seemed to be nothing more than place markers, spared destruction only until more bricks were available. The gold-leaf dome belonging to the state capitol building bulged above its neighbors like a boil.

Edwards said, "You been away too long, Cap'n. All these places got tired of rebuilding every Sunday morning after the Saturday night fires. If you'd took that campaign money and put it in the local straw concession, you could've bought your way into the Congress without ever quitting home."

Crews in mackinaws and rubber boots were shoveling heaps of fresh snow from the sidewalks and dumping it in rain barrels on the corners; still others scraped it off the flat roofs of the businesses in long grating sweeps of their iron blades. Gas lamps stood on wrought-iron posts and a Bell Telephone office shared a wall with a store that carried toilet fixtures. There were no fewer than three automobiles parked on Central Avenue, the broad thoroughfare that divided the town into equal halves like a cake of cheese. The Menéndezes regarded the machines with jaded expressions on their round wooden-Indian faces; they were world travelers now.

St. John ignored Edwards. "We're traders with an army contract, looking for a bargain on good horses. The ones they swapped out for in Mercury City are bound to have attracted notice. Don't say nothing about strangers, or let on we're law. These fellows are like to have spread enough of that express money around to buy a heap of goodwill, on top of which it's a cattle town, and nobody here's got any great love for the railroad since it swindled them out of all that grazing land. Train robbers are quality people here." He turned in his saddle and fired a volley of rapid Spanish at Paco and Diego, who nodded and fell away in two directions, melting into the landscape at their backs; everyone knew the army didn't award contracts to Mexicans.

This time, George was paired off with Edwards, and Rawlings with Pierce; St. John went alone to the two-story brick jail with a sign in front swinging from staples reading CITY MARSHAL.

Rawlings wanted to protest his choice of partners, but kept his mouth shut; to burden someone else with the company came with the assumption of special privileges. He rode alongside the Sunday school teacher, lagging back a little; something about the man made his skin prickle whenever he wasn't within his line of sight. Pierce sat blade-straight in the saddle, as primly as a young girl in a riding habit, the reins in his left hand, leaving his right free to dangle below the butt of the Navy revolver in its scabbard.

There were two public stables, one at the end of Central,

the other a block down a side street. The hotels were on their
list of stops: One, called The Meadowlark, was on the way.
They tied up there first. The lobby was pink marble, with the
yellow-breasted hotel mascot eyeing the visitors incuriously
from inside a cage the size of a church bell. Rawlings, feeling
more unshorn and unwashed than usual, held back from the
desk in favor of Pierce; somehow he managed a regular shave
in the ghostly light just before dawn, and seemed to have an
inexhaustible store of fresh collars in his pack.

The clerk wore a bow tie, a figured waistcoat, and hair
parted in the center like a bartender's. He turned a well-
scrubbed face to the man in black. "What can I do for you,
Reverend?"

Pierce produced an immaculate visiting card from a flat
leather case tooled with his initials. It contained only his
name, engraved in glossy black ink. He introduced himself
as an army chaplain running an errand for his commanding
officer and asked if any of the guests might be interested in
discussing a sale of horses for an upcoming training maneuver. The clerk knew of none, but promised to show the card
to the current registrants.

"The Lord's blessings upon you, sir."

THE LUCKY CHANCE LIVERY was painted across the front of
the weather-beaten wooden building on the side street, the
U fashioned after a horseshoe. The broad barn doors gaped
wide, one anchored in place by an iron mounting-block, the
other by a milk can filled with cement. From inside drifted
the now-familiar odor of fresh manure: warm, moist, and
welcoming rather than offensive at that frozen time of year.

Rawlings went in first this time, stepping aside for someone coming out, a squat pyramidal figure in a buffalo coat
that hung to its insteps and a well-traveled slouch hat with

the brim inverted all around. When the head turned slightly his way, he was surprised to see a round hairless face constructed entirely of bunched ovals, framed by plaits of black hair: Eyes black as watermelon seeds, with as much expression. It was an Indian woman in white man's clothes.

The sight sparked something in his memory; not quickly enough for him to react to the presence of the man standing now in front of him, wearing a khaki duck-canvas coat fastened with buttons that didn't match—brass, horsehair, and bone—denim trousers stuffed into cavalry boot tops, a hat with egg-shaped dents in the crown, stained black with sweat and missing its band, and twin revolvers strapped to his forearms with the butts removed. The arms ended in stumps without hands.

That completed the circuit. Rawlings' hand sliced down for the Thunderer in his coat pocket, clearing the fabric just as one of the stumps swung up level with his heart and its mate crossed the man's chest in a raking motion, striking the gold coin welded to the exposed trigger and discharging a slug from the barrel.

Rawlings didn't know if he got off a round. The one he took burned his flesh and struck him numb to his thighs. An umbrella opened inside his head, stopping his ears, dulling the sound of another shot close by. There might have been a third, but either it was farther away or it was something he was hearing from under water, after which . . .

Something alien invaded his nostrils and filled his head like a blast of desert air, hot and infused with alkali. His eyes grated open, exposing themselves to light so bright he heard his pupils shrinking from it. Close on the invasion came that same sense of an umbrella spreading in his skull, and with it a dull ache, as from too much bad whiskey. And then he identified the source of the assault: Someone was waving an open bottle of spirits under his nose.

It was Burt Fabian's special blend, confiscated from the medicine show he'd ejected from Pinto Creek. He reached up a hand to push it away. White-hot pain lanced up his side. The umbrella began to close and he felt himself drifting back into black nothing.

When his eyes opened again they fixed on Irons St. John's face, brick-red, baked from both sides as in a kiln, down from the sky and up from sand and snow. The coarse black hairs in his moustaches struck a contrast with the white stubble on his cheeks and chin. His eyes were faded nearly as pale as the whites.

"I'm thinking you should lop off your right hand and strap that baby Colt to your wrist like Jim Shirley," he said. "You'd be ahead. I seen Scotchmen spend less time getting their purse out of a pocket."

Rawlings swabbed the inside of his mouth with a tongue like a trout; it was no good for communication. He let his eyes ask the questions. They'd rusted in their sockets. He was lying on his back in a room lighted by a lamp that didn't reach as far as the ceiling; it had only seemed bright after hours of darkness. The sharp smell of kerosene mingled with burning wood (a heating stove), dry leather, wet rubber, and that homely spoiled-molasses odor of dung that had greeted him as he'd approached the Lucky Chance Livery; that, more than what St. John had said, was what took him back to where he'd left off: He'd been shot by James Blaine Shirley, a veteran crippled while trying to dispose of an unexploded Spanish mortar in Cuba and now a known member of the

Buckner Gang; Rawlings' old Records Division at Pinkerton's maintained a mutually beneficial arrangement with the War Department in Washington.

"We're in the tackroom behind the stables." Straightening, the marshal's upper body joined his head. Thick sinew jumped in his forearms as he rolled his sleeves back down to his wrists. He still wore the rough wool pullover he'd had on in the private parlor car at the beginning of the expedition— years ago, it seemed, when the world was in its cradle—its appearance unimproved by countless days without a wash. Rawlings didn't suppose his own appearance was any treasure.

St. John shrugged back into his sheepskin coat. "I'm sorry to tell you that you won't be mustering out of this here outfit for a clean bed and a mistress of mercy to tuck you in it; you're still of some use. That ball took a rasher off your ribs, but when it comes to needle and thread I could find work as a lady's maid if I ever run out of bad hats to chase, and I'd stack my dressings up against any field hospital in the U.S. Army. Gunpowder and chaw does the healing. There's *soldados* giving Mexico City hell right now that would've been feeding the coyotes in Chihuahua twenty years ago if I didn't use 'em for practice."

The flesh on his right side drew tight when he stirred. The pain raced up his ribs, but he felt the stitches pull and hold. "How—?" Separating, his chapped lips made a splitting sound, louder than the word itself.

The lawman misinterpreted his meaning. "You'll be back on your wheels tomorrow. It's why I didn't call for a doctor. He'd put up a fight—fever, infection, carbuncles and tapeworms—and I need all the fight I got to deal with Race and Merle. They jumped the fence after what happened to

Shirley. You can't say they didn't get their money's worth here; the news came with a couple of horses behind the Cowboy's Rest where they was staying."

Rawlings swiveled his head an eighth of an inch from side to side; the cornshucks—or whatever the pillow was stuffed with—rustled. This time St. John understood.

"You're asking how is it you're still this side of the sod. Pierce. Drilled Shirley and his squaw both before you hit the ground. She come up from behind with a knife that made that Bowie you inherited look like a spoon. You never saw a sharper blade in a smaller fist."

He closed his eyes, projecting the scene onto the backs of his lids (*The Marvel of the Century!*): the Sunday school teacher drawing and firing from savage instinct, then spinning on his heel to kill the Indian woman who stood in for Shirley's hands. Whether the story of the knife was true, and whether her wound was in front or back, was immaterial now.

His head was lifted; a calloused palm rubbed against the grain of his hair. Something prodded at his mouth. He smelled alcohol again, opened his lips this time to accept the neck of the bottle. The raw stuff burned a trough down his throat. He coughed, but managed to resist choking; he seemed to be acquiring a tolerance for rotgut. His head was lowered. He kept his eyes shut and let the heat find its way to the paralyzing pain.

"We'll move you to the hotel tonight: the Meadowlark. It's close, and the bed's got springs instead of a plank. I had to argue your way into this one here, but that won't last. A sick horse counts for more than a wounded man in this place. I'll send somebody back with grub. Getting shot's good for the appetite."

He opened his eyes. "What did you do with Shirley?"

Just then an edge of gelid air knifed between boards. The lamp glowed fiercely, illuminating the ceiling. It was lower than it had seemed back when it was swallowed in darkness. Harnesses hung from the walls, stirring in the icy current. St. John was standing near a lopsided door with his hand on the strap handle. "It'll keep," he said, grinning. "We won't even have to take down a door. He'll be stiff enough to stand up on his own. You can take his boots off if you want."

10

12:16 LARAMIE

As it happened, the mortician, a small sandy Irishman who looked as if someone had tried to drag him through a knothole by his nose, awarded James Blaine Shirley all the attention of a leading citizen upon his departure from this plane. (Rawlings suspected a discreet arrangement with the city marshal in return for favoring his establishment with the burial contract over his competitor. A notorious bandit on public view guaranteed a steady flow of curious observers through the parlor at a nickel a head.)

For photographic purposes the double amputee was stood before the shop in an octagonal coffin with his arms folded across his chest in an *X* to display the matched Colts secured with leather straps to the stumps, wearing a frock coat provided from the company stock and the Bronze Star he'd been awarded for action in the war with Spain strung by its striped ribbon around his neck. (It had been found wrapped in a bandanna in a pocket of his bloody khaki tunic.) The coat, and the position of the arms, concealed the mortal wound. With his eyes shut and his sparse ginger whiskers trimmed into neat imperials, he looked like a wounded officer recovering in hospital.

He retained his boots. There was no mistaking the identity of *this* deceased, with or without measurements.

Leaning against George American Horse for support, Rawlings snapped the shutter a second time and asked the mortician what had become of Shirley's companion. Frowning, the mortician led the pair through the perpetual twilight inside to a room behind the business offices, the Pinkerton balancing himself between George's arm and a stick promoted from the Starlite Saloon: a bamboo crook the bartender used to measure the beer remaining in a keg.

Here, nothing had been done to preserve dignity in death; the place, in fact, was almost affectedly practical. It was a plain workshop, stripped to the essentials: tools, benches, jars and tins containing anonymous compounds on crude shelves, an evil-looking device that resembled a pump. Their breath steamed; the room was unheated. The air swam with alcohol, ammonia, and—as expected, but not really prepared for—the stale-flesh reek of the charnel-house.

The Navajo woman whom Shirley had depended on to act as his hands lay on two planks placed across a pair of sawhorses, demonstrably naked under a burlap rug. Her face was bloated, eyes and mouth left open. It was ancient, of a kind unseen in 10,000 years except painted on rock; yet it was unlined. Her hair, unbound now, fanned out on the planks, shining wet, with silver glittering in the black like the filament in an electric bulb. The water bucket used to sluice down the body stood on the floor between the sawhorses. No other preparation for burial had been made.

Rawlings didn't ask the location of the wound.

"What will happen to her?"

The Irishman pulled his nose, as if it might retract to its original shape. "Marshal's getting a wire off to Wind River; but if the Shoshones on the reservation don't take her, there's a plot of land we use for indigents on the railroad right-of-way. It just sits there, doing nothing but be owned by the railroad."

"No markers?"

This drew only a puzzled look.

"What else did you expect?" said George, when they were outside.

"I thought you might say something."

"I was to start doing that, I'd never get anything else done. Ike wants us at the hotel. Can you handle it, or do you need to go back to your room?"

The Cowboy's Rest occupied a portion of town that had so far survived the steady crawl of brick construction up Central Avenue. It was two stories of clapboard, with the uniquely Western addition of a third floor that extended no more than six inches back from the street, supported by two-by-four braces, with tall windows opening onto nothing but blue sky. It appeared to exist only to accommodate rooftop sharpshooters and extemporaneous lynchings; a relic of the cattle town's rowdy past. The front was painted yellow with blue trim, and some attempt had been made to gentrify the ground floor with window boxes planted with evening primrose, brown and shriveled like dead spiders.

The group gathered in a plain pine lobby with a wooden bench off the entrance and a bald Negro clerk behind the desk, blinking at them through gold-rimmed spectacles. Rawlings and George came in last. The Pinkerton's right side was afire, and the trek from the Meadowlark Hotel to the mortuary and then there had left him light-headed and perspiring, but he reserved his complaints for himself. Twenty-four hours ago he'd lain bleeding in the dirt.

"Where's Testament?" St. John said.

The others looked around as if one of them were hiding Pierce. Edwards didn't participate.

"Church, he said."

"Which one?"

"Lutheran, I think. The white one."

"Is it Sunday?"

"Can't be. I didn't hear bells."

"We'll talk. The Lord's not running this outfit."

The clerk started to lead them to the second floor. St. John stopped him long enough to poke a coin into his pencil pocket. "You ain't seen us, son." He'd been unimpressed with the local representatives of the law.

George took Rawlings' arm, but he shook it off and followed up the stairs, gripping the banister. He passed the clerk coming back down to his post, rattling his arsenal of keys.

The Pinkerton leaned on the doorframe while the others wandered the room. A heap of wrinkled sheets lay in a corner. The Buckner brothers had tied the linens together to make a ladder and checked out by way of the window. The room had been left undisturbed by the staff; St. John had prodded the city marshal into giving that order. The man was an obstacle by nature.

"I didn't know better, I'd swear we was in the presidential suite of the Palmer House," Edwards said.

It was a low-ceilinged room with two beds, a plain wardrobe and chest of drawers, a braided oval rug, and a framed print of a snow-covered Valley Forge that looked exactly like the scene outside the window. A lamp had burned out on the narrow night table; the city gas lines had yet to reach the neighborhood. All the rooms on that floor shared a bath down the hall.

"It was the smart choice," said George. "Some of the local element might wonder how a bunch of saddle tramps traveling with an Indian woman wound up in a toney place like the Meadowlark. What might they have in their saddlebags? They'd have to defend themselves on two fronts; the law on one side, their own kind on the other."

A yellow-backed novel with a painted Indian on the cover lay curled like a leaf on the table. St. John picked it up, riffled the rough-cut pages and abandoned it, his sixth sense hit-and-miss as usual. He sat on one of the stripped beds, took off his hat, and rumpled his grizzled hair. He was wearing his years today and more: There were satchels under his eyes and a crust of cigar left unattended in a corner of his mouth.

Edwards jerked open the door to the wardrobe. A faded flannel shirt sagged drunkenly from a wire hanger inside, nothing else. They'd made a clean sweep in a hurry.

"That colored clerk didn't know nothing about an injun woman," he said.

"They wouldn't put her up here any more than the Meadowlark," said George. "He didn't remember a guest with stumps where his hands belonged neither. Shirley needed her day and night, so they likely both curled up in a corner at the livery; which is how Rawlings and Pierce got to make their acquaintance in that place."

He was helping search the room as he spoke, opening and shutting drawers, pulling Valley Forge from the wall to look behind it, dumping out the wicker trashcan and sorting through the crumples of paper on the floor with the toe of his boot. He went down on one knee to spread open newspaper pages (finding no circled items), shake loose some torn scraps clinging inside the can, and match them to others on the floor. He tried arranging them in several configurations before they formed a rectangle of ruled notepaper with even sides, then paused.

"Ike."

He gathered the pieces carefully, rose, and reassembled them next to St. John on the bed. Pierce, Edwards, and Rawlings came near to read over the marshal's shoulder. The scrawl was faint, hurried, made with a blunt, hard-leaded pencil:

142 12:16 Laramie Dec 4

St. John consulted the faces around him. "We still in November?"

The rest looked at one another; all except Rawlings, who reached for his current notebook. It was with his revolver in the right-hand pocket of the mackinaw he'd borrowed from the livery to replace his ruined coat; the side where he'd been wounded. He gritted his teeth as he drew out the book between two fingers, then switched it to his left hand and paged through it. Each entry was accompanied by the date it was made. He stabbed at the most recent—11/27, the day before he was shot—with his forefinger. "Just barely. It's the twentyninth; Thursday." He nodded at Edwards.

The marshal started to turn his head Rawlings' way, then switched to Wild Bill. "Run down to the train station and bring back a timetable."

The Pinkerton had been relieved, if only temporarily, of his assigned duty as errand boy for the posse. He supposed he had Shirley to thank for that, at least.

"It's a ghost train." Edwards flung a rectangle of stiff gray cardboard onto the bed.

St. John put his hat back on; a sort of coronation, Rawlings thought. Without it, his shag of hair, thinning at the crown and grooved evenly all around where the hat settled, carried no more authority than a panhandler on the street. He seemed to grow in stature when it was in place. He left the railroad schedule where it was.

"Meaning the train's a ghost," he asked Edwards, "or ghosts is all it carries? I liked you better back when you didn't talk so much. When you did you made sense."

"Meaning there is no twelve-sixteen, not to Laramie nor from it. I asked the stationmaster. He looked at me like I'd growed a second head. He said he knows that timetable like Solomon knew the Queen of Sheba and there never was no train come through Laramie at that time, midnight nor noon, since he had the job, and no Number four-oh-two. They built the station around him, to hear him tell it. He looks it, too."

"You talked to him, why bother bringing the timetable?"

"I knew you wouldn't believe me if I didn't. We don't get along so well as we done."

St. John blew a gale of air. "Don't pay no attention to that, Bill. I turned fifty this year, and that's all I'll say about that. I thought we had something finally: Being ahead of the Buckners would be a nice change. Mebbe Race left that note behind just to curdle our brains more than they was already. It'd be like him. Merle's no good for nothing but company."

"Maybe he wrote it down wrong," Rawlings said.

"And he's made so many mistakes. He tore this one up out of embarrassment."

"I'll wire Agency headquarters. Their sources run higher than stationmasters."

"Have 'em send the answer to Laramie." St. John picked up the timetable, looked at it, and stood to stretch. Bones crackled like burning straw. "We been up since Tuesday—if this is Thursday—all except Rawlings, sluggard that he is. I thought we might sleep under a roof for a change, mebbe pick up the trail from a night in Race's bed, but there's a train to Laramie at two-forty. It's as likely a place as any to ask Race about his trash. Let's go roust Pierce out of his devotions. If he ain't square with his God by now I reckon he never will be."

11

GOD'S HOUSE

Wary, perhaps, of divine retribution, progress had spared Trinity Lutheran Church from demolition and reconstruction. It stood, wooden and alone, between the Lonetree Emporium and the office of *The Cheyenne Leader,* both of recent brick manufacture. The saltbox structure, painted uncompromisingly and uniformly white from its foundation to the great iron bell in its steeple, professed silent faith in God's mercy, armed against fire and a rapacious century.

The party dismounted in front of the building; all except the Mexicans, who sat as always with their carbines at ready rest and no expression on their faces. Rawlings didn't know where they'd come from, hadn't seen them until the group had mounted for the ride from the hotel; they'd just materialized from whatever billet they'd made for themselves outside town, without being summoned. They came and went like smoke.

A triangular roof—an echo of the steeple—covered the front porch at the top of six steps. City Marshal Eugene Welk, red-faced and clean-shaven under a Stetson hat with a ribbon band, stood in its shelter facing the newcomers, feet spread and thumbs hooked inside the armholes of his vest. This exposed the ivory handle of a big American revolver in a shoulder harness and his badge of office, an elaborate shield, gold-washed and suspended by tiny chains from a scroll-shaped bar pinned to his breast.

"I never knowed it to fail," St. John had said when he'd first laid eyes on Welk; "take any Saturday-night sinner, hang a junk-wagon on his chest, and overnight you got yourself a six-foot case of piles in a ten-gallon hat."

Nothing had intervened to change that first impression. It was reciprocal: Two killings their first day in town had eradicated all doubt.

"Gentlemen." The other man on the porch addressed himself to St. John. "I'm Pastor Dismas. Mr. Welk tells me the man inside is your associate." The angular cleric's white collar separated his black cassock from his bronzed church-picnic face as if his head were floating free of his body. The wind whipped his mane of hair into a white flame.

St. John removed his hat. Welk followed his lead, his face crimsoning further. Pink scalp showed through a lemony haze. St. John said, "I'm obliged to take your word on that, Padre. I can't see through walls."

"It's your man Pierce." The city marshal had a thin, piping voice: an asset on a public platform, but not in a position of command. "I've got a warrant for his arrest." He displayed a stiff sheet of paper headed in Old English lettering; holding it in four fingers by the top, as if a crease would destroy its authority.

St. John held out a hand and waited. After a pause, the other descended the steps and surrendered the document. St. John set his wire-bound spectacles astride his nose and read. He unhooked the glasses, folded the sheet into thirds, and slid it inside his coat.

"I wonder, does a lawyer work a farm the way he writes a writ, chase a chicken ten times around the barn and expect it to fatten up? I learned enough bastard Latin in Parker's court to pass the bar in all forty-five states. How much is the bail on preaching without a license?"

"He'll sing his psalms to the devil soon enough. I wired his name and description to every state and territorial capital between here and Sacramento. He rang the bell in New Mexico and Nevada. He's wanted in Albuquerque for raping a fourteen-year-old girl and they want to ask him questions about a twelve-year-old in Sparks."

A sole scraped the pavement. He swung his attention to Rawlings, who opened and closed his hand on the crook of his stick, a conciliatory movement; it had nearly slipped out from under him.

St. John said, "It was kind of you not to pull him out of his covenant and throw him in jail. Or was you waiting for us to come along so it wouldn't cost you the parson's vote?"

"I got two men at the back door and another in the alley in case he comes out the window. They know what to do. He showed what he's made of yesterday."

Dismas made a croaking noise in his throat. "That stained-glass window came all the way from St. Louis! The parishioners paid for it with donations. There isn't another like it in the country."

"That's out of my hands, Reverend. Unless his friends care to go in and talk him out of that rebel sixgun and into a pair of Yankee handcuffs."

Edwards said, "Shouldn't take more than one of us to even the odds: One man against just four of the locals might leave the town with nobody to keep the peace."

"We *had* peace till you chased them Buckners here like weasels into a henhouse. Three days later we got two strangers shot down in the street and a child rapist in our church.

206 ● LOREN D. ESTLEMAN

We'll build us a gallows one last time, say thank you for your help and don't come back."

Edwards drew breath. St. John held up a hand. "That's enough, Bill. Always happy to help out a brother officer, Marshal." He put on his hat, caught the eyes of his companions, and jerked his head toward the church.

Welk stood aside to clear the steps. "He's at the altar, praying his way into hell."

"Just tell your men to hold their fire. All that stained-glass." St. John climbed the steps.

Dismas stood his ground at the top, hands swinging loose at his sides. His bunched chin was whorled like a walnut and looked as hard. "It's God's house, gentlemen."

St. John stopped on the next step down, his men strung out below him, Rawlings balanced between his stick and the wooden railing with his left hand in the pocket of the mackinaw, where the Thunderer rested; it was his off hand, but the pain was too much on the right.

"There won't be no trouble, Padre." St. John turned his head just far enough to take in his men. Edwards lowered the muzzle of his heavy rifle.

"You forgot these." Welk rattled a pair of bright steel manacles. St. John ignored them.

"Hats off, boys. You heard the pastor."

The four ascended with heads bared. The Menéndezes backed their horses around one-handed, barrels raised, stationing themselves at the church corners, covering the entrance from both sides. Dismas vacated the space to join Welk in the street, outside their field of fire: the city marshal fisting his revolver, the minister fingering the cross hung around his neck.

The paneled doors formed a cathedral shape joined in the

center. At St. John's nod, George American Horse grasped the iron handle of the one on the right and swung it open, moving backwards with the thick oak performing as a shield. The others were spread out along the top three steps, pistols drawn; all except Edwards, who stood dead center aiming at hip level; at this range, a bullet from the chamber of the rolling-block would plow through meat, muscle, and bone and bury itself in a wall ten feet behind the target. It was built for buffalo.

Time stood on the balls of its feet, waiting for a report from inside the building. None came.

St. John dipped his head again. Clothing rustled as the group moved in, closing to fit through the doorway.

Inside, there was quiet; the rise and fall of the wind stopped at the threshold, along with the varied creaks and thuds and shouts of town life a thousand miles away. Afternoon light slanted in through tinted panes set at angles in the Renaissance window. The image was of St. Sebastian, tethered to a post and bristling with arrows, his mouth frozen in silent agony. They were creeping through a revolving barrel made of colored glass, the colors shifting constantly with the play of shadows: men moving, the passage of clouds across the sun. Rawlings twisted this way and that, the gun in the wrong hand, dizzy with pain and fear, haunted by the memory of a flaming muzzle in front of him, of a born killer behind him.

Who was behind him no longer.

Two rows of scrolled wooden pews extended the length of the room with an aisle separating them. Empty hymnal racks shaped like lyres were attached to the backs of the seats. The aisle ended before a padded rail at the base of a wooden pulpit. Above this hung a full-length portrait of Christ in His

final torment; trapping the congregation in the crossfire between martyrs. A man in black knelt on the rail, shoulders
tented, the soles of his boots exposed.

He wasn't praying alone.

12

TIME PIECE

Another pair of boots was aligned with Pierce's; small ones and more delicate. Slight as he was, his companion was doll-like in comparison, with auburn curls spilling down her back. She wore a cloth coat with a fur collar and her soles were barely scuffed: dressed for town, and possibly a visit to a house of worship.

Without waiting for a signal, the four late arrivals split up to approach the rail along the narrow passages next to the walls, moving slowly to diminish the creak of floorboards and rustle of clothing; but the room was an amphitheater and their quarry's hearing preternatural. He was on his feet, facing away from the altar, so quickly Rawlings couldn't swear later whether he'd seen him move, the Navy .36 in his hand as if it had always been there. Suddenly the room rang with the sounds of movement: The rattle of Edwards' rifle as it came level, hammers crackling; Rawlings' last because of his clumsy thumb.

"Stand down, Testament!" St. John's shout shook dust from the rafters. "We can talk this through."

The Sunday school teacher stood in a crouch, the octagonal barrel of the Colt in a plumb line with the center aisle: A twitch left, a twitch right, and a bullet would reach any other man in the room. He'd removed his hat to pray, resting it on the rail. His hair looked sealed to his scalp. Rawlings realized then he'd never seen the man blink. He might have been born without eyelids, like a fish.

The girl was still on one knee, but she'd turned on it to expose her profile: a snub nose, a bulbous forehead, a round chin, pale lips parted showing white teeth, eyes round as poker chips in a face still clinging to its baby fat. Her flat chest was pumping. She wore ankle-length fur boots with peach-colored bows on the insteps. The Pinkerton couldn't help staring at those little boots.

"Pierce, it don't feature." St. John's voice now was gentle. (How many personalities could one man have?) "You got six rounds against two dozen. You always was tidy: You don't want Rawlings taking your picture with your shirt full of holes. Jail ain't so bad, and you can always get out. I know what I'm talking about."

Rawlings felt something, a change in the current of air. He was standing behind George, across the room from St. John. The Indian was moving. Or perhaps not; he couldn't trust his senses. The progress—if it was that—was glacial.

Pierce's instincts were animal. He swung the pistol George's way. George froze.

The room stopped turning. Even the clouds outside the window seemed to have pulled up short.

A beat; then the tension went out of Pierce's shoulders. He rose from his crouch, spun the pistol, and held it out toward St. John, butt foremost.

The lawman closed the distance between them and reached out with his free hand, taking possession of the Navy. He had a gun now in each fist, like a desperado on the cover of a dime novel. On him it looked natural.

Backing away, he caught Rawlings' eye and hitched his head toward the girl half-kneeling on the rail.

Rawlings understood. He uncocked and pocketed his revolver and crossed between the rows of pews to the other side of the room.

"Tell Welk it's over, Bill. Tell him call in his dogs."

Edwards went back out through the front door. There was an exchange, the words lost in the gulf between the porch and the altar.

Rawlings stood over the girl, offering his hand. She looked at it uncomprehendingly, like a squirrel staring at a suspicious nut. She snuffled and hiccuped, choking on tears. She started to rise, stumbled; he stepped in, catching her by the arm. She was surprisingly heavy, as if her bones had dissolved and the only thing keeping her from sprawling was his hand on her wrist.

"Take her out the back," St. John said. "Make sure it's clear."

Rawlings heard a furious clicking, like someone tossing pebbles at a window. It was the girl's teeth chattering. Her skin was ice cold to the touch; she was shivering in spite of her coat. Dropping his stick, he took off his borrowed mackinaw, wrapped it around her like a blanket, and curled his arm about her waist to help her up the three steps to the pulpit platform. He could feel her trembling through the coarse wool. The effort of supporting her, and the flaming pain in his side, made his head swim; the umbrella was closing once again. He took his lower lip between his teeth and concentrated on putting one foot before the other.

There was a door at the back of the platform, nearly invisible in shadow. He opened it just wide enough to look out, to right and left. The street behind the building was empty. Steps led down to it: The building was filled with steps. They took them together. A brick building stood on the other side, blank but for a door that gave access to a trash barrel. He patted the girl's elbow and reclaimed his arm. She started across, stopped, looked back at him. He didn't know what sort of look he gave her in return. She stumbled forward, found her footing, and went on, without looking back again. His last impression was of a tiny figure lost in folds of red-and-black check, entering the narrow alley that separated the building from its twin next door; sobbing still, but more quietly.

He couldn't bring himself to re-enter the church to retrieve his stick. He took the alley that ran alongside it to the front, steadying himself with a hand against the wall, the other holding his bandaged side. It was damp, whether with blood or sweat he couldn't tell; it was a wonder how much a man could perspire in freezing cold.

Welk and three men Rawlings didn't know stood at the base of the porch, surrounding Pierce and St. John, who placed the butt of the Navy in the city marshal's hand. Pierce had put his hat back on. The strangers wore badges on their coats: plain stars, without chains or scrolls. They carried repeating rifles. Two wore moustaches, one with a curly beard attached, but they all seemed to bear a family resemblance to Welk: the same red face, the same scuttle-shaped jaw. George and Edwards stood off to the side, their weapons still in hand. The tension was febrile; heightened, the Pinkerton thought, by the ever-present mounted Mexicans with their El Tigre carbines and a crowd of civilians straining for a better view from across the street, without putting themselves in the line of fire.

Welk produced his manacles and barked at Pierce to hold out his hands. The wind tore his thin voice to shreds. Pierce's was a full octave lower, addressing St. John.

"Hold my watch for me," he said, reaching for the gold chain that crossed his vest. "I don't trust these godless men who would violate holy sanctuary."

The street shifted from under the Pinkerton's feet.

He was back in the private parlor car at the beginning of the manhunt, watching the Sunday school teacher cleaning his weapons, including an odd derringer that resembled a dollar coin.

His own gun was in his hand; he didn't remember drawing it. At that he was slower than St. John, who fired his big Colt at point-blank range, setting fire to Pierce's vest, almost square in the center of the pocket from which he'd pulled the little pistol attached to his watch chain.

"'The Protector.'" St. John read the legend stamped on the back of the trick gun. A bit of chain still clung to it; broken when it was jerked from the dead man's hand. "Them smiths back East know how to tell a joke. I seen it a couple times, but I didn't know where he kept it. Not till it was almost too late for Marshal Welk."

Edwards said, "It was me, I might've slowed down some."

"A lawman's a lawman, fancy badge or no. And I wasn't sure but that he had another shot. Who'd be next? I didn't dislike Welk enough to take the chance."

The sandy Irishman who ran the mortuary wasn't paying attention to the conversation. He was looking at his latest customer, pulling at his nose in thought (Rawlings decided that was definitely how it got that way). Midian Pierce lay across the sawhorses in the workshop. The Navajo woman had been removed, probably to cold storage in some woodshed pending an answer from the Wind River Reservation about her disposal. The dead man looked even smaller stripped of his coat and vest, a scarlet sunset staining his shirt three inches above the belt. His eyes, wide open as always, showed no less emotion than they had in life.

"I can't do better than ten," said the mortician, leaving his nose alone. "That's without embalming or a monument. He's got to have a box and caulking; that's town law. Can't have him leaking into the water supply."

Edwards spat into the sawdust at his feet. "We didn't bring him here to dicker. You told George and Rawlings the railroad right-of-way does nothing but be owned by the railroad. Plant him there."

St. John shook his head.

"He was one of us. He could've shot any of us in the church, but he saved it for somebody else. This ought to cover it." He handed the Irishman Pierce's derringer. "Some cattleman's widow might buy it to pin to her bodice."

The little man took it and held it close to his face.

St. John said, "Well, don't bite it. It only looks like currency."

A braying noise invaded from outside, warped by the wind. They'd missed their train; but then they'd regarded it as lost as far back as the church.

"He'll hate not being read over," Edwards said. "He'll haunt us sure."

"He haunted us when he was alive." George struck a match off the corner of the dead man's jaw and set flame to a cheroot. The head rolled to the right. "What will become of that girl?"

St. John took the twist of tobacco from between George's lips and put the glowing end to a cigar. It caught. He stuck the cheroot back where he found it and blew smoke at the corpse.

"Don't say nothing about her to nobody. She don't exist. Pierce must've smuggled her in through the back when the padre stepped out to talk with the marshal. Whatever he done with her or didn't is between her and her folks, and maybe Dismas. That's if she says anything at all. I'm not paid to care one way or the other."

Rawlings shivered, missing his coat. He thought of the girl making her way from the church. He would always think of her as Our Lady of Trinity Lutheran.

1926

Dr. Titus took the stethoscope from his ears and folded it in both hands, rattling the tips. He was absolutely hairless down to his eyebrows, but his scalp didn't shine like those of other bald men. It was as dry as an egg in its shell.

"Chest pains? Shortness of breath? Fatigue?"

"No, yes, and yes." Rawlings buttoned his shirt.

"Well, I shouldn't have to tell you to pace yourself and take plenty of rest. Your heart rate's still not what I'd like. How's your supply of tincture? You know, you must take that in small amounts. It's dangerous stuff."

"I have to take everything in small amounts; even poison." He shook his head, smiling tightly. "I've barely tapped the bottle."

Titus drummed his fingers on the stethoscope's diaphragm. He didn't appear to be listening. The Clinic staff tended to place research ahead of treatment; the patient's complaint was more important than the patient himself.

Had Rawlings suspected that, he'd never have made the move to Rochester.

"If you were to ask my opinion," Titus said—"and you're the only patient I've ever had who never does—I'd say your troubles started with that amateur medical treatment you received in Wyoming. It was performed under septic conditions by a man without training, and he got you out of bed too soon. I think it's directly related to your history of rheumatic fever, which should have taken its toll on your heart much sooner. Frankly, I don't know how you survived that first week."

"I'm not sure I ever did."

13

IF NOT YESTERDAY, THEN TOMORROW

They swung west at Lodge Pole Creek, a frayed thread of black drawn through the snow on the road to Laramie, midway between Horse Creek and Cheyenne Junction. The junction—no connection to the city of Cheyenne, which they'd left behind hours ago—was an afterthought on the part of the Southern Pacific, and a carbon copy of Elephant Crossing; even the prairie-dog town might have gotten swept up with that obsolete settlement and reconstructed at the next end-of-track.

A dusty orange sun was extinguishing itself in a snowy saddle between bluffs. It drew no clouds with it; they'd all decamped to Colorado when the wind wheeled south. Now there was nothing between the riders and frozen outer space. The cold pricked their nostrils, gnawed at their joints, and Rawlings, at least, felt that his earlobes would break off if he touched them with a finger. These were the conditions that existed when they made camp for the night.

The fire they managed to kindle from brush lining the creek heated little more than itself. They laid their bedrolls as close to it as possible without setting them afire and rolled into them, separated from one another by inches only, to share body heat. The Mexicans made one heap under their blankets. Rawlings, lying near enough to George American Horse to feel his breath on the back of his neck, understood then how rumors got started about the all-male situation on the frontier, and didn't care. Those who spread them had never spent a night in Wyoming on the cusp of December.

Footsteps creaked in snow dry as ash and St. John settled down on his other side, giving himself up to gravity with a grunt. He brought with him a gust of wood-smoke, coarse tobacco, stale sweat, and sour mash—smells shared by the others in the party, but which Rawlings would always associate with the marshal—and with it a welcome sense of warmth. The man came with his own climate, like a planet.

The Pinkerton sat up too quickly, gasped—and reached automatically for the bottle extended his direction. George muttered something in a guttural tongue and turned over, taking the blanket with him.

"Did you leave any for Sheriff Fabian?" Rawlings wiped his mouth and returned the bottle, the glow anesthetizing the pain in his side. The bandages were fresh, the skin still tender from its brief exposure to the cold.

"He's a barber, don't forget. Bay Rum ought to hold him between medicine shows." St. John swigged, looked at the label in the frozen light of the stars; they were as big as pocket watches. "I read somewhere this stuff is slow poison. I guess that's so. I been drinking it almost forty years and it ain't caught up to me yet."

Someone chuckled. The sound surprised Rawlings, in no small measure because it came from himself. "Not exactly what they served in the sampling room of the Acropolis Hotel in Bismarck."

The marshal's laugh was astonishingly youthful; but then he'd made such rare use of it.

"That place almost cost me my star. It wasn't like Old Thunder to expect any better when he pinned it on me."

Rawlings took back the bottle, drank. He let the whiskey pool in his throat before committing it to his stomach.

"Why didn't you give me up to the others, about Cheyenne and the rest?"

"On account of you lied? If I was to take a switch to you for that, I'd have to dust my own britches first. Wherever you started out from, whatever you done—robbed a widow, killed a man, burned down an orphanage, even cheated at cards—you can come out here and say you was the Governor of Delaware; and who's to call you out, the man who says he drunk French champagne from Jenny Lind's slipper? Let it go. It ain't like I lost sleep over it, considering what little I get anyway. And it turned out all right. We're short a man as it is."

"The world's no worse off for that."

"He wasn't much company, and that's the truth."

"That's not what I meant."

"He saved your life."

"I was just something standing between him and Shirley. Six inches to the right and he'd have fired straight through me."

"One second later and we wouldn't be having this talk. Your trouble is you don't appreciate the sun when it shines on your ass. It don't often."

"He didn't have to shoot the woman; even if she did come at him with a knife, which I doubt."

"She knowed what she was getting into when she took up with Shirley. If it wasn't Pierce it would've been somebody else, if not yesterday then tomorrow, or the day after that. We're all of us born to rot in the ground, some sooner than others. I should've been dead in Mexico, or in that livery in Miami, or on Parker's gallows, or in front of Sam Crosstree's outhouse in the Chickasaw, or a parcel of places since; but

I reckon the good Lord had plans for me. There's probably something in Testament's Bible about just what, but he ain't here to quote it."

"You knew about Pierce; you hinted as much once. Was he worth it?"

"You wouldn't ask me that if you spent any time in the Nations; what they was till Parker got his teeth in, and even after, though he left his mark. Man is a wicked creature, and that place was made with him in mind. There's times I'm grateful to Alaska for what it done to my sleeping. When you're awake all night you don't get nightmares." He tipped up the bottle, swallowed; shook his head. "No's the answer. But I didn't have proof then, just things I saw off to the edge. A man can talk himself into plenty when he won't turn his head to look the devil in the eye."

"What makes a man like Pierce?"

"Too much time with his nose stuck in just one book."

Rawlings waited for more, but nothing came. The wind had died down; the silence made his head throb. He wondered if the others were awake and listening. Again, he didn't care. He wondered why tonight was so different.

"Your bullet didn't come anywhere near his heart, but he was dead in minutes. I didn't think that was possible."

"Nicked his liver. He only lasted as long as he done out of spite. He was long on that."

"He had the gun in his hand, and you shot him before he could use it."

"That wasn't sporting, I own. Next time I'll give him the first move."

"You miss my meaning. I could never react that quickly, no matter how much practice I had on the range. Something would make me hold back."

"You were quick enough when he went for his watch."

"Not as quick as you."

"I wish I'd never learned how to work a trigger."

A strange thing to say.

The bottle came Rawlings' way again. He shook his head. St. John poked the neck into his raw side. He cried out.

"Smarting, are you? Hair of the dog."

"You son of a bitch." He took the bottle and drank.

"No, sir. I am the son of Thomas St. John, who was nobody's son. He blowed in on a bad wind and took root in a horse apple. I'm a hitch better than him, and if that deacon in Idaho's my boy, I hope he's a hitch better still, because if he turns out like Pierce I'll hunt him down and make him a capon." He corked the bottle and stood. "I best be getting back to Wild Bill. He'll be turning blue by now."

"You're more than a hitch better."

But St. John was gone; and afterward the Pinkerton wasn't even sure he'd said it aloud. He hoped he had, whether or not he'd been heard.

IV

HOME FROM THE HILL

1

PIPE DREAM

It was late by the time he got back from the clinic, and he had to twist the bell to be let in. Sofia, Mrs. Balfour's housekeeper, unlocked the door. She was a Hungarian with a bad eye he couldn't help staring at; it was brown with bands of blue and green, like agate. The tall cabinet clock against the wall read half-past eleven: It bonged once while he stood on the threshold. Sofia told him—in a tone that left no doubt as to where she stood on the issue—that he had visitors waiting in the parlor.

The room, off the foyer behind heavy curtains hanging from ivory rings, was in transition; whether forward from Victorian or backward from 1926 depended upon the war of wills between the landlady and her daughter-in-law, a creature of the twentieth century. A console radio shared the space with plush furniture, and a Deco rug done in emphatic primaries competed for attention with framed samplers whose homely bromides reminded Rawlings uncomfortably of Midian Pierce's preferred reading. The air smelled of lavender and cigars; the space was a common room used by the boarders to entertain guests.

Buck Jones rose at his entrance. The cowboy star had come out of his cocoon: He wore tall boots tooled with his initials, a string tie with a fawn-colored blazer, and the hat he held in one hand had a great curled brim, a towering crown, and a beaded band; he looked ludicrously out of place and comfortably at home at the same time.

His companion remained seated. Tonight, Joseph P. Kennedy was in a midnight blue single-breasted, with vertical stripes this time on his silk tie: Just because his tastes were conservative, it said, it didn't follow that he was a slave to convention. His owlish glasses reflected a floor lamp with a fringed shade in both lenses, masking his eyes. Rawlings wondered if he'd chosen that chair with the angle in mind.

A cigarette slurred smoke from between the second and third fingers of the Bostonian's hand. He drew on it, then reached over to crush it out in a tray on the table at his elbow.

"I apologize for the hour, Mr. Rawlings. I had a meeting in Minneapolis and it ran longer than expected. Mr. Jones was kind enough to alter his plans accordingly. We met by arrangement at the station. He's here to scout locations for *The Last Manhunt* up North; hiring an aeroplane for the purpose. It seems he's as daring offscreen as on."

"My wife says I'll take one too many chances someday." Jones stepped forward to offer his hand.

Rawlings took it. "She may be right. I didn't know the project had progressed as far as that. I haven't heard anything since I sent you the latest pages." He was looking at Kennedy.

"I preferred to discuss them in person. I could have scheduled that meeting in Boston, but since the party has offices here I found that even more convenient. Mr. Jones is restless. There's talk in Washington that the moving-picture business has gotten out of control and a committee must be appointed to prevent more scandal like the Arbuckle trial and the Taylor murder. He's eager to push his project through before congress shuts down Hollywood. I've assured him these things blow over; but when you're young, every disaster is something that never happened before and must bring down ruin on us all."

"We're the same age, Mr. Kennedy," Jones said. "And you don't know Hollywood. The industry's new, and unsure of its strength. The studios are apt to jump the gun and shut themselves down before Washington can move in, hoping to avoid worse, and bring about the worst instead."

"Well, the trip is your investment. I haven't pledged a penny beyond what I've authorized." He looked at Rawlings. "We can postpone this until morning if you're tired." He glanced at the watch strapped to his wrist. His actions struck a balance between subtle and overt.

"Not at all." Rawlings was exhausted, in fact; but he suffered from the sick man's need not to acknowledge weakness in a business situation. He took a seat facing the visitors, shedding his coat and placing his hat on the floor beside the chair. Jones returned to his chair and sat with his hat in his lap. He looked like an immigrant seeking permission to enter the country; once again, Rawlings suspected he would cut quite a different figure back in Los Angeles. Meanwhile Kennedy seemed to be at home whatever his surroundings: a true citizen of the world.

"You wrote 'The End' at the bottom of the last page we read," said the Irishman. "But you left Race and Merle Buckner still at large. It's a story without a conclusion."

"It always was. Without its leader, the manhunt lost momentum, and when the Buckners lost Jim Shirley, they hadn't the numbers to continue. The theory at Pinkerton's was they split up and fled to Mexico along separate routes to make them harder to track." The unspoken one was that Rawlings was somehow responsible for an open end to a costly (and embarrassingly public) investigation. For that crime he'd been buried to his elbows in the monolithic file cases in the Agency basement to wait out his pension.

For lack of positive information, rumor rushed in to fill the vacuum. In 1910, Race Buckner was seen simultaneously in Matamoros among the revelers celebrating the Day of the Dead and in London, packed in with the crowd outside Westminster Abbey trying for a glimpse of the coach bringing George V to his coronation. A more plausible account reported Merle Buckner's death during the attempted robbery of a payroll train bound for a sugar refinery in Vera Cruz; eyewitnesses insisted he was drunk on pulque or he wouldn't have attempted to shoot his way through a *federale* patrol. A party of Pinkertons (not including Rawlings) went down to investigate both Mexican stories on a commission from the railroad, but the natives in Matamoros were openly hostile to gringos and uncooperative, and none of the people the detectives spoke to in Vera Cruz could or would tell them where the attempted train robber was buried, or even corroborate any of the stories. A peasantry in a constant state of revolution formed protective circles around bandits, even imported ones.

Paco and Diego Menéndez quit the posse in Laramie when no trace could be found of the Buckners; when George, Edwards, and Rawlings left the Great Plains Hotel to meet with them in the Mexican quarter, they were told "*los hermanos*" had ridden out during the night. The others weren't very much surprised: The absence of Irons St. John clearly indicated that the paying work had come to an end. Although a Menéndez was reported slain in Chihuahua during General Pershing's ill-advised expedition in 1916, this too could not be confirmed, and at all events the surname was common in Mexico. The pair had simply been swallowed up in the deserts south of the border (if indeed they'd gotten that far), along with hundreds of others who had chosen the life of the brigand.

The reward that had been offered upon proof of James Blaine Shirley's death never came, no surprise: In all his time with the Agency, Rawlings had never known such money to be paid. There were always accountants to claim it had all been spent on the investigations, with figures to back them up.

"That ghost-train business had potential," Kennedy said, "yet that, too, was abandoned."

Rawlings said, "The significance didn't reveal itself until long after the events. The train was an express from Denver to Washington, D.C., with its first water-stop scheduled in Laramie at twelve-sixteen A.M., an unusual time; but it was an unusual train. Officially it didn't exist. It was commissioned to transport several million dollars in uncirculated bills from the Denver Mint to the U.S. Treasury, and was kept a secret for years, until the run was canceled in favor of other arrangements. How the Buckners found out about it we may never know, but it's a fair bet the information cost them most if not all of the eleven thousand they cleared from the robbery in Elephant Crossing; you may remember they destroyed nine thousand in securities in Mercury City because they were too easily traced. If so, it was a bad investment on their part. An army regiment was aboard, guarding the shipment. The gang hadn't the firepower necessary to take it on, with or without Shirley; with or without the Army of the Confederacy, comes to that. It was a pipe dream, but they couldn't resist following it up."

"It's absurd, I agree. Still . . ." Kennedy lit another cigarette and waved out the match; a wistful gesture.

Buck Jones was looking at him. "It's not a serious omission. We can supply an ending. All audiences care about is that a train is robbed, not how much is taken. There's a majestic stand of old-growth ponderosa in the Chippewa National Forest that would make a honey of a spot for a horseback chase and shootout."

Rawlings had witnessed that very scene projected on a bedsheet in Colorado, with a prospector maniacally squeezing his concertina in a desperate attempt to drown out the rain drumming the corrugated roof overhead. Had nothing changed in the moving-picture business in twenty years? So much had, everywhere else.

He didn't address that; he was no expert. He said, "You would improve on history, then: Punish the wicked with death and raise the good from the grave. I didn't realize we were writing a morality play."

The actor uncovered those unlikely teeth. "Well, of course. The studios will have nothing else, especially now. I have to deliver the goods in the last reel. I'm the Iron Star, after all."

You're more than that, Rawlings thought. *You're Lazarus.*

2

FIRST LIGHT

"Carve it deep, George."

"Waste of time," George told Edwards. "The first blizzard will blow it to hell, and the spring runoff will wash away the rocks and him with it. Coyotes will see to the rest."

"He won't mind. He was as much at home out here as them; a hell of a lot more than behind some desk in Washington. Carve it deep just the same. It ain't like we got anything better to do."

"I doubt he'd agree," George said. "He never took a penny he didn't earn."

"Not counting what he stole," said Edwards.

"So he said. He was the biggest liar you'll ever know."

Rawlings watched, hugging himself in the Arctic cold. He'd awakened at first light, shaken out of a jumbled dream by a foot on his shoulder. The foot belonged to Wild Bill Edwards. Edwards had been startled, instantly awake, by a change at his side; in that climate it didn't take long for the heat to leave a dead body. He'd peeled aside St. John's blanket to look at the gray-blue face, frost bleaching the fringe of his lashes and moustache. The marshal had drifted away in the dark.

"Heart, I guess," George said. "First time I knew him not to put up a fight."

Edwards said, "It ain't fair. He didn't ride for Parker all them years to die in his sleep like some damn ribbon clerk."

"We're all of us born to rot in the ground," Rawlings said.

They looked at him.

The Pinkerton helped to gather rocks, using his heel to kick some loose from earth frozen too hard to dig a hole; it rang like iron when struck. George borrowed Carroll Underwood's Bowie—Rawlings' souvenir—to cut pine boughs to tie together to form a cross and carve the name of the deceased and dates of his birth and death; Rawlings supplied those from his notebook. They didn't move the body, disturbing it only to turn it onto its back, then securing the blanket around it to create a shroud.

A flat bottle slipped out of his pocket while they were turning him over.

"How many of 'em did he have squirreled away?" said Edwards.

"I think this was the last." Rawlings picked it up and slid it into one of his own.

George said, "Saving it, maybe."

They assembled the rocks on top of the corpse, piecing them together like masonry, and jammed the cross as deep into the earth as it would go.

Edwards blew on his hands, rubbed them together, and produced something from under his coat. Rawlings recognized it by the oblong strips of paper sticking out from between the pages.

"Where'd you get that?"

"Took it off Pierce. He don't need it no more."

Rawlings snatched the Bible from him and flung it away in the same movement. It opened as it flew, fluttering its pages, scattering its bookmarks, and buried itself in a drift without making a noise. "Not that book."

"He'd want reading over."

"Not that book." Rawlings was wearing the coat he'd procured in Cheyenne to replace the mackinaw, a shapeless thing of scratchy wool that fastened with wooden toggles. He drew out the bottle, threw the cork over his shoulder, drank, and passed it to George. When it reached Edwards, he took a shallow swig and poured the rest over the grave. The liquid splashed over the rocks, found its way into the tight spaces in between, and vanished, steaming a little as it went.

"Hair of the dog, Cap'n."

They saddled up and rode on to Laramie. No word was said about it; it was where they'd been headed, and there was no one now to order a change in the plan. Riding away from it, Rawlings pictured Pierce's Bible, undisturbed from where it had fallen, bloating in the rain and snow, the pebbled cover peeling away, the onionskin pages withering, coming apart, blown to hell by the wind. There was nothing holy about it, the uses to which it had been put. The whiskey was more honest, even if it was disguised as medicine. Hair of the dog.

3

NOT COUNTING MEXICANS AND INDIANS

The cabinet clock in the foyer struck one. The gong seemed to go on long after it had ceased to echo in the stillness of a sleeping household. Rawlings was physically drained, but his pulse was racing so fast he felt himself vibrating in place. The long train journey from California had taken a similar toll on Buck Jones, who sat slumped in his chair with his hands gripping the arms as if to prevent himself from sinking deeper into the cushions. Only Kennedy seemed fully alert; but the retired Pinkerton observed that the spent butts in the ashtray had constructed a log jam that might collapse if just one were removed from the pile.

"I'm still interested in the project," Kennedy said, lighting another off the stub of the last. "Some things must go: Pierce, the degenerate, most certainly. If anything were to poke the sleeping bears in government, it's sexual deviation; and the Catholic Legion of Decency will never sit still for a man of the cloth thus engaged."

Did he cross himself at that point? Rawlings was yawning, and unable to trust the evidence of his eyes. Kennedy went on before it could register. "We'd be caught in a pincer movement between Washington and the Vatican. No one could survive that."

"'Banned in Boston'?" Rawlings lacked the energy to keep irony from his tone.

Kennedy's glasses flashed his direction.

"You wouldn't joke if you'd seen it in practice. I never enter into a speculation until I've done my research. Every city, village, county, township, and parish in the country has a tin-pot czar in charge of censorship who answers to no one, and they all take their marching orders from the Bishop of Boston. Mr. Jones?"

"It's true. MGM was forced to shut down a major production because a toilet appeared in one scene."

Rawlings lifted a hand, letting it go. He only wished Midian Pierce could be as easily expunged from his memory. "You said 'some things' have to go. What else did you have in mind?"

"St. John's checkered past, of course," Kennedy said. "We've touched on that. The czars would insist he atone for his crimes. Death from natural causes won't satisfy them; that's out in any case. He must be alive at the end of the film, after bringing all of the Buckner Gang to justice. The man Wild Bill: same thing there, something shady in his past. Let's see; what else did we discuss?" He looked at Jones.

"The Mexicans."

"Yes. The subject is too controversial so soon after the Villa assassination, and the War Department is still sensitive about that debacle in Mexico following his raid on Columbus. The country entertained an alliance with the Kaiser during the world war: All it asked for in return was Arizona, New Mexico, and Texas! And of course there's the question of race. As it stands now, the white men in the posse are outnumbered. The Mexicans must go if we're to keep the Indian."

"I wasn't aware there was any problem with the character of George American Horse."

"Not if we get rid of the Menéndezes," Jones said. "Bull Montana would be my choice, if we can get him away from Paramount."

"Bull? You mean like Sitting Bull? Is he an Indian?"

"Italian, I think; but he'll look terrific in a loincloth. Even his muscles have muscles."

"George didn't wear a loincloth. He dressed like the rest of us. Otherwise he'd have frozen to death in a Wyoming winter."

"Oh, we won't be shooting in winter. The film freezes in the camera: *Way Down East* almost ruined Griffith. Principal photography won't start before June. Even then Minnesota poses risks, so if the budget will allow it, we'll have some sets standing in Burbank for studio exteriors." He overcame his fatigue enough to put his dentalwork back on display. "We used to be pretty provincial, we movie people; we started in a greenhouse in New Jersey. Now we're getting to be a Gypsy lot, always on the move."

Rawlings drew nothing from that. Burbank sounded like a city in Australia; but Jones's concern with budget argued against that.

"Everybody out here came from someplace else. Not counting Mexicans and Indians."

He was muttering. Kennedy's brows rose above his frames. "I'm sorry?"

"Unimportant. Something someone said once." To Jones: "Are there no Indians in pictures?"

"Too much red tape—so to speak. Most of them are wards of the government, on reservations. The Department of the Interior's hard to work with. Also, Hollywood's a hard-drinking crowd; and that's the mildest of its vices. The red man has no tolerance. By the way, does your landlady keep liquor in the house?"

"We've trespassed on our host's time long enough." Kennedy uncrossed his legs. "We're done here, I think. You're free to do what you like with your book, although if we proceed with *The Last Manhunt,* we'd appreciate mention in the publicity."

They'd reached the end of their association. Rawlings couldn't tell if he was disappointed or relieved. He got up to see them out.

His heart was working fast enough to beat him to the top of the stairs. He hung up his coat and hat, took the tincture of coal-oil from its pigeonhole, laid aside the eyedropper, and sipped straight from the bottle, measuring what he considered the proper amount in the action. He stripped off his waistcoat and tie and laid his watch and chain on the desk. (It always reminded him of Midian Pierce and his hideaway gun.) He pulled down the bed and stretched out without bothering to remove anything else except his shoes.

Sleep eluded him, as usual. He watched the play of shadows on the ceiling: nocturnal industry on the part of bats and moths tempting death for the temporary solace in the heat of the bulb in the streetlamp outside his window. They combined in a pantomime of past acquaintances.

George American Horse had volplaned away from his life after Laramie. A cutting from *The Cheyenne Leader* had passed through his hands in Pinkerton's Records section had made note of an Indian who'd conducted interviews seeking the location of an anonymous Navajo woman's grave on the

Southern Pacific right-of-way outside the city, but neither the little Irish mortician nor anyone else he spoke with could identify it specifically. Rawlings liked to think it was George, hoping to re-inter a fellow native in a proper grave; but it might just have been a representative from the Wind River Shoshone Reservation following up on an inquiry made too far in the past for local memory to furnish the necessary information. However, *some*one with the Agency must have had some reason for filing the article, and if not because it was connected with a member of the posse it had assembled to apprehend the Buckner Gang, what was it?

Wild Bill Edwards had spent a season with Pawnee Bill's traveling Wild West exhibition, demonstrating his sharp-shooting skills during a stop in Sacramento, but Rawlings hadn't made the journey from San Francisco to take it in: What would they talk about, if not the episode that had cost the Pinkerton a permanent promotion to field agent? It was a post he no longer prized, but he would have liked to have had the opportunity to turn it down. The show went bank-rupt in 1910 and Edwards—whatever his real name was, and however he had come into St. John's sphere—passed beyond Rawlings' ken.

But Rawlings remembered the six of them—St. John, George, Edwards, the Menéndezes, and himself, camped out on the floor of an extinct farmers' mercantile on the barren site of Mercury City, passing around a pony bottle of uncured whiskey and listening to one of the marshal's tall tales, while Pierce brooded over Scripture in a corner; and for some reason he fell asleep, oddly contented.

He knew nothing more after that, or ever would.

AFTERWORD

Those familiar with *Mister St. John* (and there must be dozens!) will note a number of departures from the original plot, particularly in the later events of the manhunt. I ask their mercy. The challenge of retelling the story a generation later, from the perspective of three time periods simultaneously, wrought necessary changes, both because I didn't want to swindle readers by rehashing the same events and because in forty years I've learned a great deal more about the craft of fiction and western history and was eager to invest that knowledge and spend the interest.

In shifting point of view from the original omniscient narrative, in which all things are known, to third-person subjective, in which the focus is narrowed to the personal experience of a single character (Emmett Force Rawlings), I found that some details no longer worked, and that the new format offered better ones. This approach led me into territory that was fresh yet familiar, preserving the best of the old while making the story original once again.

Race and Merle Buckner, James Blaine Shirley, his Indian helpmeet Woman Watching (unnamed here), and Llewellyn Carroll Underwood are virtually missing this time around, in so far as readers were privileged to ride the outlaw trail with them the first time. Moving them from center stage to the background gave them a mystique they didn't have before.

Except where members of Irons St. John's posse encounter the last three directly (and violently), they remain smoky figures on the horizon, swimming in a mirage, with the grueling realities of life on the run implied rather than explicit; in truth, both pursuers and pursued faced the same hardships, and all are present here, in a form I found more dramatic.

In the movie *Havana*, Robert Redford's character says, "I like Westerns. I don't know what they have to do with anything, but I like them." An odd statement, coming from the star of *Jeremiah Johnson* and co-star of *Butch Cassidy and the Sundance Kid*; but appropriate to the nihilistic atmosphere of the 1990s. In fact, Westerns have everything to do with who we are as Americans.

The genre represented a complete break from the literature of the Old World, just as the Trans-Mississippi migration after the Civil War forged a national character that's still the envy of Europe and Asia. A colony no longer, we began to *give away land*, free for the taking, neither granting it to a noble few nor surrendering it to a conqueror. No other nation had ever done that, and we created a literature to advertise our unique place in the world. Those two things, expansion and invention, united to hammer out a myth that stands beside those of ancient Egypt, Greece, and Rome, and the Anglo-Saxon legends of King Arthur and Robin Hood.

I emphasize the term "legend." What does it matter that the prearranged face-to-face fast-draw contest (to name one of the form's many tropes) was contrived by novelist Owen Wister, and absent entirely from the historical record? Mythology is built on tall tales. Apocrypha is truth in a nutshell, telling us as much about its subject in a paragraph as history does in a book.

That said, the best Westerns confront history head-on.

A society that would stage photographs using dead outlaw corpses as props—grisly hunting trophies, in effect—seems medieval, yet it was only yesterday. Generations of writers censored such disturbing details; and it's why the Western lost its dominance. After Vietnam and Watergate, who had time to waste on morality plays pitting good against evil, when it had become clear to most of us that the roles were often reversed? This is why so-called "revisionist" Westerns like *True Grit*, *The Shootist*, *Dances with Wolves*, *Lonesome Dove*, and *Unforgiven* blew out box offices and swept awards ceremonies between 1970 and 1992. They revised nothing, except the common misconception of a real period in the making of America, and audiences embraced them for their courage and candor. All but one of these films were based on novels; *Unforgiven* was inspired by true accounts. All were faithful to their sources. Audiences evolve with the times, even if some writers and directors don't, and they recognize the goods when they're delivered.

And who's to say that photographing slain criminals and publishing the photos is so barbaric? If more of today's mass shooters were thus displayed (as opposed to alive, armed, and in mid-homicidal-stride), the gory images might deter imitators, who, let's face it, are only after face time on YouTube. The building blocks of civilization are fired in crude ovens.

I don't claim that *Iron Star* so benefits our culture (social consciousness, as Vladimir Nabokov once pointed out, is not the writer's burden), or that it belongs on a list of landmark Westerns; only that what's good about it—and about *Mister St. John*, its progenitor—comes directly from the pages of history.

If this sounds pretentious, considering the genre's subliterary reputation among critics, let's not overlook the fact that a well-written Western is a thumping good read. It certainly is for me, when I revisit the work of Douglas C. Jones, Don Coldsmith, Lucia St. Clair Robson, Glendon Swarthout, and Elmer Kelton—serious artists whom it's been my pleasure to read, and eventually befriend. To them and their predecessors—Jack Schaefer, Conrad Richter, Dorothy M. Johnson, Oakley Hall, and A. B. Guthrie, Jr., to name a handful—*Iron Star* owes a debt that the rest of us can only repay by trying to uphold the same principles; without their example, the Western might have vanished a half century ago when CBS canceled *Gunsmoke*.

—Loren D. Estleman
April 18, 2023

ABOUT THE AUTHOR

Deborah Morgan

LOREN D. ESTLEMAN has written more than eighty books—
historical novels, mysteries, and Westerns. The winner of
four Shamus Awards, five Spur Awards, and three Western
Heritage Awards, he lives in central Michigan with his wife,
author Deborah Morgan.